A
CANDLELIGHT REGENCY SPECIAL

Candlelight Regencies

The Magnificent Duchess

SARAH STAMFORD

A CANDLELIGHT REGENCY SPECIAL

Published by
DELL PUBLISHING CO., INC.
1 Dag Hammarskjold Plaza
New York, N.Y. 10017

Originally published in Great Britain by Milton House Books
under the title *The Gay Gordons*

Dell ® TM 681510, Dell Publishing Co., Inc.

ISBN: 0-440-15371-9

Reprinted by arrangement with Delacorte Press
Printed in the United States of America
First Dell printing—June 1977
New Dell Edition
First printing—November 1980

Chapter One

"Do not argue with me, Georgiana! We are going to Woburn, and that is that."

"But I do not want to go to Woburn, Mama."

Angrily Georgiana stabbed her needle into the tapestry she was working, pricking her finger as she did so. She put it into her mouth to ease the pain, making further argument impossible. The duchess continued unchecked.

"Are you setting yourself against me, miss? Remember what a pother you made about my wearing the tartan to Queen Charlotte's drawing room when I presented you? And which of us was right? *I* was, of course!"

Georgiana winced as she recalled her dismay at seeing the duchess preparing to go to court with bouffant panniers of Gordon tartan over a yellow satin underskirt and her lace lappets tied with tartan ribbons.

Rising from her chair, the Duchess of Gordon strolled over to preen herself in a long gilt mirror while her daughter, still sucking her finger, remained silent.

"Surely you didna' expect me to wear white, Georgy? White's for debutantes—och, it's many a year now since I wore virginal white, if ever I should have done."

The duchess's chuckle made Georgiana shrug her shoulders in irritation as she caught the words she had probably not been intended to hear. If only Mama did not say such outrageous things! Had she no delicacy at all?

With a final twitch at her skirt, the duchess reluctantly turned away from the mirror and wagged a reproving finger at her daughter.

"That's all forbye now. You've had a very successful season, thanks to me, and now we are going to Woburn. Must I remind you that it is impossible for us to refuse the Duke of Bedford's civil invitation—and I dinna' want to, in any case. It's the fashionable thing to be in his house party for that sheep-shearing festival of his, not that I'm interested in sheep but, as well ye ken, I'm one of the most fashionable women in London. Indeed, I canna' think why I was never invited before."

Georgiana removed her finger from her mouth and said wearily, "Yes, Mama, I know you're fashionable, but I am not."

"And what is more," the duchess retorted, "unless you do as I say, you never will be."

"But I have not the faintest wish to be fashionable! If you want to go to Woburn, why can you not go alone? Why must I go with you? Is it because you are on the catch for the Duke of Bedford?"

"Georgiana Gordon! Don't be vulgar! I canna' think where you get your ungenteel expressions."

She was suddenly conscious that Georgiana had picked up her language from her, and added hastily, "I am not, as you inelegantly put it, 'on the catch' for anyone. All that concerns me is that you should be suitably married, like your sisters. Now, no more tantrums, please."

"That is most unfair! I'm not in a tantrum. I'm perfectly cool." Georgiana's flushed face belied her words. "Of course, it is my concern, very much my concern, whom I marry."

"Ye're blethering, girl. It is not becoming for a chit like you to lay down the law about whom she is to marry. Wait until I tell you I've had an offer for you."

"You know I've had a number of offers," Georgiana retorted hotly, "and you also know, Mama, that I've taken a fancy to no one. Nor, it seems, have you—at least, you haven't tried to push anyone on to me. It's no more than natural that I should want to know if you have someone in mind for me *and* still more whether I shall like your choice! All my sisters were married during their first season, and mine has now ended without my even being betrothed. I do think I am at least as handsome as they are—and nearly all my friends are bespoken and I am not!"

Georgiana's loud sniff as she voiced her complaint was intended merely to annoy the duchess. Since as yet she had met no one whom she felt the slightest inclination to marry, only her pride was hurt. What was the good of being the prettiest girl of the season if her friends, none of whom could hold a candle to her, had already walked off with all the matrimonial prizes?

With a heroic effort, the duchess held her peace. Lately her daughter's temper had been so uncertain that even the most oblique reference to a match for her was capable of producing an outburst.

Georgiana, too, gave up the impossible struggle of crossing swords with her mother, but as the time of their departure for Woburn drew near she observed with naughty satisfaction that the duchess was increasingly twittery. Ten times a day she gave contrary instructions to her groom of the chambers, Matthias Damour, until even his usual imperturbability was ruffled.

"Yes, indeed, Your Grace. Your Grace has already given me her orders about the traveling carriage and the horses—several times. I think Your Grace knows that she can safely leave the arrangements to me."

And Damour had bowed himself out of the duchess's presence.

Deprived temporarily of the opportunity to tease him further, the duchess turned her attention to her daughter.

"You're looking pale, my love—a little rouge will not go amiss. And look at your hair. It's all out of curl. Ring for Damour."

He came, wearing a martyred expression.

"The horses, Your Grace . . ."

"Ach, never mind the horses—if they've got four legs, they'll take us," exclaimed the duchess impatiently. "See to Lady Georgiana's hair."

Damour took a comb from his pocket, flicked at Georgiana's curls, then stepped back several paces to examine his handiwork with a critical eye.

"Her Ladyship's curls are perfect, as always, Your Grace. Now, if Your Grace will excuse me, I shall not be available for the next hour or so. I am going to the stables to—to count the horses' legs."

As Damour withdrew with an air of finality, the duchess ignored the impertinence, knowing that once Damour had given an ultimatum, he would allow nothing to disturb him until he appeared again of his own free will. It was always wise to let Damour do as he wished. He was the best servant the duchess had ever employed. Since she had found him in Edinburgh, threadbare and almost starving, he had been the prop and stay of her harum-scarum household. From dressing hair to dancing the hornpipe, there was nothing Damour could not do, except satisfy her curiosity about his origins.

"Tell me, Damour," the duchess had asked imperiously on first engaging him, "how does it come about that with so many accomplishments you have been reduced to this pass?"

He had hesitated a little before answering quietly, "I am an *émigré* from France, Your Grace. I was fortunate enough to escape from the excesses of the revolution, and, until I can return to my unhappy country, I shall be content to remain in Your Grace's service."

"But who are you—who *were* you?"

"I am Your Grace's obedient humble servant to command."

"Yes, yes, I know you are now, but you haven't answered my question. Who were you in France?"

Damour had smiled gently.

"Your Grace will surely allow me to keep my own secrets, as she may be sure I shall keep hers."

And, however much the duchess teased him thereafter, he would say no more, leaving her imagination free to roam at will about his past life, although she was convinced he had been a personage. So courtly was his manner, so urbane his demeanor, that he must be an aristocrat, a duke in disguise at least, forced to menial employment to keep himself from starvation.

"Ye ken," Jane Gordon confided to her intimates, "Damour would make a far better duke than Alexander. He has such an air, and my husband has no air at all! You might think Alexander one of his own crofters. Give him a horse, a dog, and a gun, and that's all he cares about—shooting and stalking. If I did what Alexander wanted, I'd be cooped up forever in Gordon Castle with only red deer and grouse for company, and nothing to look at but gloomy forest. Alexander's welcome to live on a diet of Scotch mist, haggis, and the doggerel he's so fond of writing, so long as he doesna' expect me to share the feast. Whoever speaks of the Duke of Gordon? Nobody! Who speaks of the Duchess of Gordon? Everybody!"

The duchess's frequent complaints about her husband were a poor recommendation for marriage, Georgiana felt, but marriage was her mother's obsession. It was impossible for her daughter to rid herself of the teasing suspicion that the object of their visit to Woburn was to arrange a match.

Certainly, by the time the Gordon ladies were due to leave for Woburn, the duchess's state of nerves had almost succeeded in ruffling even Damour's habitual calm, while Georgiana herself was nearly driven to mutiny. All through the drive she huddled in a corner of the carriage, obstinately refusing to take the smallest interest in the pretty little Hertfordshire villages through which they passed along the Great North Road. She allowed an air of disdain to steal over her face, and with patent disinterest she plucked at a thread in her pelisse while the duchess thrilled over the Duke of Bedford's wealth and greatness.

"Bedford is one of the largest landowners in the country, and one of the richest—almost as rich as your papa —and, although he is a Whig, he has a very proper sense of his obligations. Mr. Pitt told me . . ."

Ostentatiously Georgiana stifled a yawn and turned her back, to look out the carriage window. She might have guessed it would not be long before her mother had dragged her favorite topic into the conversation.

"Mr. Pitt told me that the duke made a freewill gift of a hundred thousand pounds towards the cost of the war, all swallowed up no doubt in subsidies to those Austrians! And what must they do after all the help we've lavished on 'em, but make peace with Bonaparte. Och, I never could abide foreigners—you canna' trust them—Sassenachs are bad enow."

"Damour's a foreigner, Mama, and you trust him." Georgiana's voice was studiously sweet.

"Don't draw red herrings, Georgiana. I'm talking about our miserable allies and Francis Bedford."

"I know you are, Mama, but you're wasting your time. I don't care how rich the duke is. I do not like him. The Duke of Bedford is not at all like Papa, and Papa is *my* idea of what a duke should be."

The duchess bit back the retort hovering on her lips. Of course, it was perfectly proper that Georgiana should have a fondness for her father, but to set Alexander up as a model was nothing but foolishness. Her mother was well aware that she did so mainly to annoy. Little minx! She'd have a word to say to her in due season.

Between Georgiana's hostility and her mother's irritation, the atmosphere in the carriage was charged with tension, boding little good for the outcome of their visit to Woburn Abbey. Georgiana's nature, however, was too sunny to allow her to sulk for long. In the hope of wiping the heavy frown from the duchess's face, she at last broke the silence.

"Will Lady John Russell be at Woburn, Mama?"

"Since she lives in the Abbey and never comes to town, I have every expectation that she will be, but I gather she rarely leaves her own apartments, so it is unlikely we shall see much, if anything, of her. Poor John Russell! He made a bad bargain when he married Georgiana Byng to oblige his family."

"Oh, is Lady John's name Georgiana too, Mama?"

"Yes, her name is Georgiana," snapped the duchess, "but I canna' see what that has to do with anything."

This show of temper again silenced Georgiana, so that when they at last caught a glimpse through the trees of

Woburn Abbey and the carriage turned into the park by the London Gate, the duchess heaved a long sigh of relief. Another minute of Georgiana's subtle rebellion would have driven her mad!

"Well, here we are, and for the Lord's sake do remember your manners, Georgiana."

"I do not think, Mama, that you have ever had cause to complain of *my* manners" was her cold answer. Damour handed Georgiana out of the carriage at the principal entrance to the Abbey and gave his hand to the duchess. As she surveyed the building critically, she forgot her annoyance with her daughter and whispered, "I must say, I've seen many ducal mansions more imposing than Woburn Abbey. How oddly it is sited, to be sure."

Georgiana was spared any need to answer, as the door was opened by a footman, and in the background they saw a stately housekeeper ready to welcome them and show the new arrivals to their rooms.

As they followed her up the narrow winding staircase, the duchess was too busy looking about her with eager curiosity to remember to harass Georgiana.

"If this is the principal staircase, it is very mean," she whispered, but when the housekeeper had curtsied herself out of the first-floor suite assigned to the Gordon ladies, she deigned to approve.

"Very proper—these are obviously the state guest rooms. I must say, I like this Chinese wallpaper. It's very similar, do you not agree, Georgy, to that in the Chinese room the prince has had decorated at Carlton House? I have a mind to a Chinese room myself when next I refurbish Buckingham House."

The duchess's running commentary went unheard. While she made a minute inspection of the furniture and the hangings, Georgiana stared out of the tall windows overlooking the park. She heard the sound of cheers from a

8

distance but, in all the crowd around the booths and pens set up near the house, she could not distinguish a single familiar figure.

"Georgy! Come here!" called her mother. "Did you ever see such an oddity? A bath which is reached by a ladder, and a bronze bath at that!"

But Georgiana had no interest in baths, and while the duchess chattered on she stayed at the window.

"The housekeeper says that forty guests are expected for the house party, and even the great stable block is hard put to it to accommodate all the horses and carriages. Georgiana Gordon, you are not listening to me! And this is no time to be idling. You must awa' to dress."

Slowly Georgiana turned away from the window, to be hustled by her mother to her own room.

"You're to wear the new white muslin, my love, with a blue sash and a blue fillet in your hair, just like Romney's portrait of me as a girl. Ye'll mind I was known as the flower of Galloway, will ye not?"

Georgiana vouchsafed no reply to this familiar refrain. The duchess paused to look at herself in the tall pier glass.

"Maybe Jane Gordon has blossomed out a bit since she was young Jenny of Monreith who was always setting Edinburgh on its ear with her capers, but she is still held to be an uncommonly fine-looking woman," she murmured with satisfaction. "Although maybe, with two sons and five daughters, I shouldna' be thinking of my own looks."

Georgiana squirmed. *Must* Mama always harp so much on herself as a young girl and a beauty? Admittedly, she was still very handsome, but her daughter found it hard to believe that the duchess had ever had a figure as trim as her own. Over the duchess's shoulder, since she was still planted full-square to the mirror, Georgiana peeped at her own heart-shaped face and merry blue eyes.

9

"Awa' wi' ye now, Georgy. Time enow to admire yourself when ye're dressed."

But when the duchess, resplendent in a new gown trimmed with the Gordon tartan, bustled into Georgiana's room, she found her still in her traveling dress, looking dreamily out the window. With difficulty, Jane Gordon held her tongue. Georgy was a good girl, but she could be as obstinate as a pig, and in her present mood she might easily be upset and do or say something to wreck the good impression her mother wished her to make.

Georgiana's maid was so overcome by the duchess's nervous fussing that all her fingers seemed thumbs, but at last the finishing touches had been put to her mistress's hair and dress.

"Move Lady Georgiana's sash a little more to the left, Kirstie—nay, you fool, to the *left*. Aye, that's it. You look simple and sweet, my Georgy. You make a bonny picture —a little more bosom would not come amiss, but it will —in time."

The duchess gave Georgiana an approving pat.

"No one can fail to see the contrast . . ."

"Contrast to what, Mama?"

Looking slightly confused, the duchess made no reply, leaving Georgiana guessing what had been left unsaid— not that she really cared. All she wanted was for this week to end quickly, because, in spite of her mother's strenuous denials, she was certain that the duchess intended the Duke of Bedford to fall into her net, a prospect she herself found wholly distasteful. She took a little satisfaction from knowing that she had done her best to make him dislike her in return. Perhaps after all he liked her no more than she liked him.

Comforted a little by this thought, Georgiana dutifully tripped after the duchess by a secondary stair into the Long Gallery, where the guests were assembling before dinner. As Lord John Russell came eagerly forward to meet them from his post at the entrance, Georgiana's face brightened.

"I must beg your indulgence for my brother, ma'am." He addressed the duchess, with a smile for Georgiana. "He was detained at the plowing match to present the prizes. I am sure his arrival will not be long delayed and he will make you his own apologies. In the meantime, please accept mine on his behalf."

Lord John had time only to kiss the duchess's hand and bow over Georgiana's before he was obliged to turn away to greet a new arrival, and she had the opportunity to look about her. Her attention was immediately caught by a very showily dressed lady with a bodice cut almost indecently low who was coming toward them.

"Is that Lady John?" Georgiana whispered to her mother.

The duchess turned to follow Georgiana's eyes, and a look of cold hauteur settled on her face.

"*That* Lady John?" She made no attempt to lower her voice, and one or two guests in her vicinity smiled. "I should think not! Georgiana Russell may be a tiresome malingerer, but she *is* a lady born! That's Nancy Parsons, or Lady Maynard if you like, one of the commonest creatures in London!"

"Then what's she doing here at Woburn? Is she related to the Russells, Mama?"

"Related to the Russells? Nancy Parsons!" The duchess was scandalized. "Scarcely! Her only relationship is to the duke, goddamn her."

As Georgiana's eyes opened wide, the duchess bit her lip, annoyed that she had yet again let her unruly tongue run away with her. Oh, these tiresome innocents! The sooner Georgy married and learned the way of the world, the better. Not that, Heaven forbid, she should be as wild as the duchess herself had been.

"Lady Maynard is the duke's housekeeper," she told Georgiana.

As Nancy Maynard continued to advance effusively toward the duchess, she gave no sign of having heard what had been said, although Jane Gordon had spoken loudly enough for anyone to hear. A curt inclination of the head was the only acknowledgment Nancy received in response to her greeting. The duchess then pointedly turned her back to engage a man standing near her in conversation.

Although she was seething inwardly, Nancy gave no sign of having noticed the cut, but she said to herself, "If you want war, Your Disgrace, you shall have it. You may think to install that namby-pamby daughter of yours at Woburn instead of me, but you'll meet your match— and not the kind you are used to. Maybe I haven't been as lucky in hooking a duke onto the right side of the blanket, nor in getting him to the church door, but I've had three dukes in my bed—Grafton, Dorset, and Bedford—and that is where Bedford's going to stay or my name's not Nancy Maynard. And, say what you will, Maynard *is* my name, even if I had to cozen my Lord Viscount Maynard into putting a ring on my finger and making me a viscountess."

Nancy's thoughts may have been vitriolic, but her face wore a honey-sweet smile as she turned to Georgiana. The girl thought she was the only witness of her mother's outrageous rudeness, but as it happened, John Russell had been watching. Hastily leaving the group to which he had been talking, he neatly interposed himself between Georgiana and Nancy before Lady Maynard had a chance to accost the girl.

Georgiana gladly accepted John's proffered arm, and together they moved away from the charged scene to stroll through the Long Gallery. As they maneuvered through the press of guests awaiting the summons to dinner, John pointed out the portraits of by-gone Russells. His pleasure in Georgiana's eager interest in his family history, however, was marred by anger at his brother. Too bad of Francis not to have sent Nancy away during this house party! Of course, the *ton* knew her to be his reigning mistress, but he fervently hoped that Georgiana did not. She was plainly so innocent, so untouched by her mother's loose talk and behavior. He wondered indeed how she had avoided being contaminated by the duchess's vulgarity and pushiness.

The thought of his own Georgiana obtruded, and John Russell sighed. He had begged her to bestir herself for once, to join the house party and take her proper place as hostess for her brother-in-law (which would at least have relegated Nancy Maynard to the background), but all he had received from her was a fretful refusal.

"John, how can you ask it of me? I do not know how you can be so wanting in consideration. Already all the noise and bustle have penetrated to these apartments and made me feel unwell. I am quite unfit to meet so many people—my nerves do not permit of any strain—and I am sure Francis would not wish me to exert myself. Go and enjoy yourself, John, since you seem to find enjoyment in these insipid gatherings. As usual, I will stay here alone and endure my sufferings as best I may."

Lady John closed her eyes wearily, but as her husband was on the point of leaving the room, she opened them again and demanded in a weak voice, "Kindly hand me my vinaigrette before you go."

John Russell was only too happy to escape from the room, where the smell of the many nostrums his wife was always swallowing gave him a feeling of nausea. Normally the most long-suffering of men, he felt that had he stayed a moment longer he would have exploded at her self-imposed martyrdom and selfishness. He reflected bitterly that he was surrounded by members of a family who thought only of themselves.

"When all is said and done," he murmured as he made his way down innumerable corridors to the Long Gallery, "I did my duty to the family by marrying to ensure the succession, while Francis, having cheerfully shucked his responsibilities onto me, amuses himself with one mistress after another. But what joy has my marriage brought me?"

His train of thought led naturally to Nancy Maynard. He hoped to God that during this house party she would behave herself, but he was only too well acquainted with her uncertain temper and the scandalous scenes she took so much pleasure in creating. How Francis tolerated her he could not understand, but he seemed impervious to her outbursts and blatant vulgarity. If Francis would only listen to him, but he would not. John recalled their last conversation, when he had begged his brother to marry.

"Why do you always insist on my marrying?" the duke had asked petulantly. "I'm perfectly happy as I am, nor have I any wish to complicate my life. At thirty-six, I'm too old to change my habits, and as I have an heir . . ."

"No, Francis, no! You're not going to get out of it that way. I have not the faintest desire to step into your shoes, as well you know. I love Woburn and the Abbey, but not to the extent of wanting it for myself alone. So long as you permit me to live there I am content, but you should marry and have some sons of your own to succeed you. As I am weary of telling you, it's your duty as head of the family, and Woburn needs, and has long needed, a mistress."

"It has one," the duke yawned.

"You mean *you* have one, Francis," was John's dry response. "That's far from being the same thing, and you know it. And you know, too, that the propriety of installing Lady Maynard at Woburn is a matter on which you and I do not and never will agree. Undoubtedly the Abbey is yours, and naturally you will do as you please there, but to flaunt your mistress in your principal seat is an affront to your neighbors and a discredit to yourself. If you *must* keep her near you," he added with distaste, "then there are plenty of houses at a discreet distance from the Abbey—at Aspley Guise or Ampthill, for instance."

The Duke of Bedford uttered an impatient sound.

"You're a very good fellow, John, if only you would not persist in moralizing. I concede that Nancy should not have been installed at the Abbey—I had my own doubts about it—but there she is, and there she will stay. You don't know what she's like when she gets her teeth into something. She's worse than a retriever."

John refrained from asking why his brother should maintain such a tiresome mistress, and Francis closed the conversation, saying, "For God's sake, let me hear no more of the duty I owe to the family. Now, I should be obliged if you would permit me to continue reading this treatise on a new method of rearing pigs—it is really of most absorbing interest."

The duke had returned to the book in his hand. John Russell shrugged his shoulders and stared out the window into the park, where the trees were showing the tender green of spring. Fond though he was of Francis, he found him very obstinate when it came to the question of his marriage.

Thoughts of Francis prompted John to another apology

for his tardy arrival and failure to welcome the duchess and her daughter.

"I trust that you will forgive my brother, Lady Georgiana, for not meeting you. This sheep-shearing festival is something very near his heart, and naturally he tries to be present at as many of the contests as possible. In his unavoidable absences, I hope you will permit me to take his place, so far as I am able. I can at least show you around the Abbey and the park."

"I shall like that very much, Lord John," Georgiana murmured softly, not displeased to exchange one brother for the other and to be relieved of any attention from the duke.

A sudden stir in the Long Gallery heralded the appearance of the Duke of Bedford. As his arrival was the signal for dinner to be announced, he had time only for a rapid round of his guests, with an affable greeting for each. The Duchess of Gordon fancied that his welcome of herself was particularly cordial, and thought that he bowed over Georgiana's hand with a special degree of warmth, so that she was in high fettle when she took her seat at the dinner table on the duke's right. For once she did not immediately engage in political argument, but allowed her host to converse on the subjects which interested him, although they bored her to distraction.

"I understand that you consider the merits of Merinos superior to those of Southdowns," she remarked brightly. In fact, she had not the smallest idea of the difference between the two breeds of sheep, but with her native Scots wit had picked up the names from the duke's neighboring landowners who were fellow guests.

Somewhat surprised, but gratified by the duchess's apparent knowledge, the duke required no further urging to launch into a long discourse on sheep, while she applied herself to the excellent dinner. At last, to her great

Georgiana tossed her blonde curls.

"So much the better. But he was so busy talking—about pigs, no doubt—that I'm sure he didn't even notice. Anyway, I don't give a fig, or a pig, for what he thinks, and you know it, Mama. As for that horrid Lady Maynard, I detest her—*her* manners aren't in the least endearing. She may be a viscountess, but she's certainly not a lady. If it weren't for Lord John, I should be having a hateful time. He is very kind to me, though."

Indeed, Lord John took it upon himself to stand in at all times for his brother, making himself Georgiana's constant companion. To her surprise, she found his attendance made watching the practice of agricultural skills far less boring than she had expected. She even became excited when the shepherds, working with amazing speed, sheared a hundred sheep in an hour, and she marveled at the arrow-straight furrows drawn by the sturdy plowmen.

Lord John's companionship may have pleased Georgiana, but it had the opposite effect on her mother, who was already nervous at the scant attention paid by the duke to her daughter. Time was running out, but as yet Francis Bedford had given not the smallest sign of fulfilling the duchess's wishes. She had hoped to avoid confiding her plan to her daughter, but with that damned Nancy Maynard so obviously on the offensive, Georgiana must be made to realize what was at stake.

"As for Nancy Maynard," the duchess said to herself as she waited for Georgiana to answer her summons, "when Francis marries, she'll disappear from Woburn bag and baggage—and 'baggage' is the right word for her."

Georgiana's heart sank when she saw how ferocious the duchess looked as she sipped her chocolate. It was a clear indication that her mother was in a bad mood. Her fears were borne out when the duchess sat up and began.

"Georgy, I'm going to be plain with you. If you have not by now guessed that it is the wish of my heart that you marry Francis Bedford, then you're more of a fool than I take you for. He will make you an excellent husband, and your estates and fortune will be greater even than those of your sisters Richmond and Manchester."

Georgiana's face crumpled, but she answered her mother bravely.

"Of course I guessed that you want me to marry the duke, Mama, however much you pretended you did not. That is why we came here, but you *know* I do not even like him, as he is so cold and so arrogant. Did you not notice the way he spoke to Damour when he came to call on us—and we all think of Damour as one of the family. Why, we girls have always called him *Monsieur* Damour. Surely you would not want me to marry a man if I do not even *like* him?"

From her expression, it was evident the duchess was becoming increasingly angry, but Georgiana rushed on nevertheless.

"And why must you talk about his wealth, Mama? As if money mattered to me! Anyway, thank goodness the duke hasn't shown the slightest interest in me, nor of wanting to marry me, and I hope he never does. I don't love him, and I never could!"

"Love, Georgiana? What has love to do with marriage? I've no patience with all this girlish romantic nonsense. You're just being coy and silly. Dukes' daughters don't marry—they make alliances suitable to their father's rank."

"Oh, pooh, I'm not a princess. I intend to marry, not to make an alliance."

Clutching at her nightcap, which was all askew, the duchess leaned forward, endangering the position of her cup and saucer, which Georgiana rescued in the nick of time.

"Dinna' put yourself forward in that unbecoming way, Georgiana Gordon, and listen to me. When I was eighteen I fancied myself in love with a young man. My papa did not approve of my marrying him because he was penniless, and Roderick went off to the wars to make his fortune so that we could wed. That was a mad scheme, though, because he had neither the money nor the influence to get himself a step up in rank."

Georgiana gazed at her mother in astonishment. The duchess, who babbled on so that her secrets were known to all and sundry, had never breathed a word about this early love of hers.

"Then," Jane Gordon continued, "your papa fell passionately in love with me, and I dinna' blame him, nymph and goddess as they called me then. Alexander Gordon was the handsomest man in the country, with a rent roll to match. The King's greatest subject, they called the Duke of Gordon. Aye, he was bonny enow, but I wouldna' hae cared . . ."

As it always did when she was excited, the duchess's Scots accent grew broader and broader, so that at times even her daughters had difficulty in understanding her. At this moment, however, Georgiana hung fascinated on her words.

"I wouldna' hae cared if he had been a *monster!* A penniless ensign is well enow if ye canna' get anything else, but when a duke offers for you it's your bounden duty to accept his offer. To refuse to marry a duke would be downright sinful."

"So," cried Georgiana, "because *you* married a duke I must. But, even if papa was in love with you, no one can say you lived happily ever after!"

"Hold your tongue, miss. That's enough impertinence

from you. I dinna' ken what young people are coming to nowadays—talking in that way to their parents. Had I spoken to my mother as you do to me I'd've been whipped, aye, and soundly, where it hurts most, on my beam. It wasna' as broad then as it is now, but that is by the way. Dinna' fash yoursel' about your Papa and me. Alexander and I manage very nicely."

Georgiana was sadly aware that whenever her parents were together they quarreled violently, and that only for appearance's sake did the duchess pay her rare visits to Scotland, but she was unwilling to provoke her mother further. In any event, she was anxious to distract the duchess's attention from the Duke of Bedford, and was curious to know what had happened to the "penniless young man," but her mother would not gratify her wishes.

For once the duchess was silent. She remembered that young Roderick had not been killed, as report had had it, but had returned from the wars to reproach her with her faithlessness, and how, at sight of him, the old flame had flared up again. A reminiscent smile crossed the duchess's face as she recalled stolen meetings in the heather, but it was none of Georgiana's business that her mother had had her cake and eaten it too! Time enough for the girl to do as she pleased when she was married, as the duchess had done before her. The only important thing was that Georgiana make the marriage her mother had planned for her. The duchess shook her shoulders impatiently, annoyed with herself for having allowed this talk of the past to obscure the plans for the present.

"When Bedford offers for you"—under the bedclothes the duchess childishly crossed her fingers, because she was by no means as confident as she appeared to be that he would do so—"you'll realize your mistake, Georgy.

It's a fine thing to be a duchess, I can tell you. And I want you to be a duchess."

Georgiana realized that on the subject of her marriage her mother was implacable, and she turned her head so that her mother would not see the tears which threatened to fall. Jane Gordon shot her a shrewd glance before she said, in a softened voice, "Nae, my bairnie, dinna' tak' on so. You'll come to see that your mama is right. You know, my love, in life there are some things one canna' have."

And the duchess sighed, thinking once again of the penniless young man who had gone so gaily to war to make a fortune to win her, and who lost her in the process.

Chapter Two

The duchess's thoughts were not happy when she was at last left alone. She brooded on the awful humiliation she would suffer if the Duke of Bedford allowed this opportunity to slip by without declaring himself. How the *ton* would laugh! Some of the guests had already left the Abbey, and her own departure could not be long delayed. The mocking gleam in Nancy Maynard's eye was more than she could bear. She was aware that her own work so painstakingly done by day could be destroyed by Nancy at night, yet she could not have mistaken the broad hint Bedford had given her when he had called after Charlotte's ball.

"Charlotte!" she exclaimed, startling her maid, who was dressing her.

"Did you want something, Your Grace?"

"No, you blethering idiot. I'm talking about the Duchess of Richmond."

She promised herself she would speak to her eldest

daughter as soon as she returned to town. Since it never entered Jane Gordon's head that she herself could be wrong, a scapegoat had to be found. Of course, it was all Charlotte's fault; she had made a mess of it from the start. The duchess dwelled on the train of events which had led to Georgiana's taking such a dislike to Bedford, and her obstinate refusal to show him the slightest encouragement, with great bitterness.

The season had been particularly brilliant, and the duchess's tartan gowns were worn almost to a thread in the dizzy round of balls, routs, and masquerades. At last the gaieties came to an end. Competition was always fierce for the honor of giving the last ball before society departed to its country estates, and this year the prize had fallen to Charlotte, the Duchess of Richmond, the Duchess of Gordon's eldest daughter.

As she and Georgiana prepared for the ball, the duchess remarked complacently to her, "Och, Georgy, I'm so happy I had the idea of sending a pattern of our plaid to China to be woven in silk. Ye'll remember that I wagered a farthing dip to your quarter's pin money that every lady of the *ton* would rush to Spitalfields to order silks woven in tartan. Lucky I did not foreclose on you! Why, even the Duchess of Cumberland complimented me —and it was after her husband, the Butcher, bad cess to him, defeated our Bonnie Prince Charlie at Culloden in the 'Forty-five that the tartan was suppressed in Scotland—until King George found he couldna' do without our brave Highlanders. How cross you were with me when I said that, if the tartan was good enough for Scots lads to fight for snuffy old Queen Charlotte in, then 'twas good enough to wear at her drawing room."

The duchess sighed.

"Now, if only I could have worn the tartan when I

presented your puir sister Madelina, maybe she'd no' have come to such a sad pass."

"Must you always call her 'poor Madelina,' Mama?" Georgiana interrupted. "I can never understand why you always do so. She's very happy married to Robert Sinclair, whom I find the most charming of my brothers-in-law, and she has delightful babies."

"Pah!" spat out the duchess. "Don't speak to me of Robert Sinclair—a baronet, a mere baronet—but Madelina would have him."

"But your own papa was 'a mere baronet,'" retorted Georgiana.

"Exactly!" The duchess was triumphant. "My father may have been only Sir Alexander Maxwell of Monreith, but *I* married a duke, while Madelina's father is a duke and she married a mere baronet. What a comedown! *And* I'll tell you this, Georgy. I may have been born plain Miss Jane Maxwell—although of course I never was plain, but a beauty—but I'll wager that the name of Gordon owes as much to me as ever it owed to your papa! And haven't three of my daughters, the Ladies Gordon, married dukes?"

"No, Mama," corrected Georgiana with a touch of malice, "only two."

"Dinna' be tiresome, young Georgy, and dinna' you dare poke fun at your mama! Ye ken well that your sister Charlotte is Duchess of Richmond, and your sister Susan is Duchess of Manchester, and Lord Cornwallis is bound to be made duke any day now, so your sister Louisa Brome will be a duchess when her father-in-law dies. Only your puir sister Madelina had to marry a baronet, just to annoy me, I'm sure."

Georgiana was heartily tired of the duchess's continual moaning that Madelina had failed to fulfill her mother's ambitions for her. With an air of innocence, belied by

waiting for the musicians to return and strike up the country dances again.

"Georgy, allow me to present to you His Grace the Duke of Bedford and Lord John Russell."

As Georgiana rose to return the gentlemen's bows with a curtsey, there was a moment of confusion as they simultaneously solicited the honor of leading her into the set which was just forming. The taller of the two then stepped back a pace, saying languidly to his brother, "Oh, I cede you the *pas*. You know how little I care for dancing."

Obviously relieved, he turned to the duchess, leaving Georgiana affronted by his rudeness. He was already involved in a fierce argument with her mother, so her haughty stare was lost on him, but her good humor was immediately restored by a pretty compliment paid by her partner as they walked onto the dance floor.

"Will you permit me to congratulate you, ma'am, on your dancing of the Scottish reels? Unfortunately, my brother and I were detained at home by urgent business and arrived only to see the last of them. I have frequently seen these reels performed on our Scottish estates at Newton Stewart but, if you will permit me to say so, never with so much grace and verve as by the gay Gordon sisters."

Gracefully Georgiana inclined her head, pleasurably surprised, because somehow she had not expected the Duke of Bedford to be so amiable. She was able to examine him more closely when they had taken their places in the set. He was shorter by half a head than his brother; his countenance was open and friendly, and she considered him in every way much more pleasing. Georgiana was sorry when the dance ended, because she had enjoyed both her partner's conversation and his dancing. As he escorted her back to her mother's side Georgiana heard her say emphatically, "And *I* tell you that it was William Pitt . . ."

From the tall gentleman's unconcealed boredom it was obvious that her mother's Tory enthusiasm was not shared by the Russells.

"I have no doubt that you are right, ma'am," said the taller Russell brother hastily as he caught sight of Georgiana, "but perhaps Lady Georgiana will now do me the honor of dancing with me."

Before she was given a chance to protest that she did not wish to dance, Georgiana found herself almost dragged into a new set, glimpsing over her shoulder a look of comic dismay on her previous partner's face. So he too realized that she had been forced into the dance so that his brother could escape from her mother's harangue!

A little spoiled by the success she had been enjoying during the season, when gentlemen had been begging for the favor of standing up with her, Georgiana seethed with annoyance at the cavalier manner in which she had been treated. Her annoyance developed into anger as her partner showed not the smallest interest in either her or the dance, which nevertheless he performed creditably enough.

Finally, when the silence had become uncomfortable, he roused himself to ask, "Are you interested in pigs, Lady Georgiana?"

"In pigs, sir?"

Georgiana's eyes grew round with astonishment at the oddity of the question; then a naughty thought prompted her. The Duchess of Gordon did not lie in saying that she was the one of her daughters who most resembled their mother. Here was an unexpected opportunity to put this supercilious gentleman in his place!

"Well, sir," she answered with apparent innocence, "my mama has told me that, as a young girl in Edinburgh, she rode through the wynds on the back of a pig. She says its squeals could be heard all down the Royal Mile as my aunt thumped the pig's backside with a pole."

The effect of this artless story was all that Georgiana could have wished. A look of pained disgust flashed over her partner's face but, whether it arose from her use of the word "backside," which was not normally part of a young lady's vocabulary, or from her mother's unseemly exploit she could not guess. Certainly, she did not care.

"I can well believe it of the duchess," was the contemptuous reply, which increased Georgiana's dislike, "but I was not thinking of pigs as a means of locomotion—a most unusual one, I confess. What I meant, ma'am, was whether you are interested in the breeding of pigs and sheep?"

"Me? Interested in breeding pigs and sheep? Good gracious, no! I can conceive no reason why I should be concerned with anything so tedious. I suppose we have all kinds of animals at Gordon Castle, but that is the factor's business, and in any event my mama and I are seldom in Scotland. She much prefers to be in town."

"That is a pity, ma'am, because I had it in mind to ask the duchess if she would honor me with a visit to Woburn Abbey. May I dare to hope"—the gentleman bowed slightly—"that you might be persuaded to accompany her? I should be most happy to show you the new strains of pigs and sheep I am rearing."

Georgiana had not looked for such courtesy from this prosy bore who could converse only of pigs and sheep in a ballroom. For a moment she was puzzled as to why he rather than his brother should have proffered the invitation, but she cared so little that the matter was immediately dismissed from her mind. She hoped only that her mother, too restless ever to stay long in one place, would not decide to visit Woburn Abbey. For her own part she could conceive of nothing which would amuse her less than being conducted around smelly piggeries and invited to scratch an old sow's back.

Her partner now seemed to have exhausted his conversation, and the remainder of the dance was performed in silence. Georgiana hoped that this pig breeder would not ask her to dance again, but her fears proved groundless. Almost before she had risen from her final curtsey, the two Russells had vanished, followed soon after by the remaining guests, until only the duchess and her daughters were left. As they sank exhausted onto chairs and sofas and eased the sandals off their aching feet, the duchess's head drooped on her ample bosom, and she dozed.

"I'm so glad you enjoyed yourself, Georgy," said the Duchess of Richmond fondly to her youngest sister.

"I did indeed, Charlotte. It was a lovely ball."

"How did you like the Russell brothers?" chimed in Lady Brome with a covert glance at Charlotte Richmond. "What a pity they arrived so late."

Georgiana wrinkled her brow.

"The Russells? Oh, you mean the Duke of Bedford and Lord John. I thought the latter gentleman absolutely insufferable—so chilly and disdainful—and you'll never guess what he talked about!" Georgiana gurgled. "Pigs! So, to shock him, because he really is the greatest bore, I told him the story of how Mama rode on a pig when she was a girl in Edinburgh. And he was shocked, as I intended he should be."

Georgiana clapped her hands in glee as her silvery laugh floated through the room. She did not see the bewildered glances exchanged by her sisters, but Charlotte said gently, "Are you sure you're right, Georgy dear? Lord John would not talk about pigs—I do not believe he takes any interest in them. You must have made a mistake—Bedford is the one who thinks of nothing but experimental agriculture. He's forever trying out new ideas at Woburn. I know this because he's always urging Richmond that he should do the same at Goodwood."

Charlotte paused, remembering now how flustered she had been by the Russells' tardy arrival. Obviously her introductions had been so hurried that Georgiana had mistaken one brother for the other. That was a pity indeed! She must do her best to repair the damage before her mother awoke.

"Georgy, you seem to have mixed up the duke and Lord John. It must have been my fault in not making it perfectly clear to you which was which. Lord John was wearing a blue coat and Bedford black—and I must say, it was superbly cut, far and away the best coat in the room. I only wish Richmond could be persuaded to go to Francis Bedford's tailor," she added brightly, hoping that the duke's sartorial magnificence would correct the bad opinion of him which Georgiana seemed to have formed, but her sister only tossed her curls.

"So far as I am concerned, handsome is as handsome does. If I was mistaken about which Russell was which, then it was the duke whom I did not like at all, not that it is significant. Lord John, then, was quite different from his brother, so delightful and kind and charming, and, although it may not be modest on my part to say so, I am convinced he admired me."

A lift of the eyebrow from Charlotte Richmond met a nod from Susan Manchester, who now intervened briskly.

"Delightful? Lord John? Are you sure, Georgy? I have certainly never known him to be so, because in general his life is a dreary one, and, of course, he is only a younger son. His wife is sickly and never goes into society, and although he is never heard to complain, she is, I believe, a great trial to him."

To hide her dismay, Georgiana bent to fiddle with her

sandal. The knowledge that Lord John was married came as a shock. He was so much nicer than his brother that she had taken to him at once, and now was a little resentful that he had not spoken of a wife. It was, of course, unimportant, but nevertheless she felt a curious disappointment, and realized that her sisters were giving her a kindly warning. At this moment the duchess woke from her nap with a great yawn and at once began to belabor the Duchess of Richmond for her temerity in featuring the Highlanders at her ball.

"Well, Charlotte," she said tartly, "you can be pleased —your ball was highly successful—but I'll no' forgive you for trumping my ace by bringing in *my* Gordon Highlanders. Ye'll mind it was *I* who did most to raise the regiment by putting a golden guinea between my lips. The lad who took the guinea took a kiss from me, too, and it was no peck, I assure you! In the highlands a kiss *is* a kiss! And one lad threw his guinea back, saying a kiss from the Duchess of Gordon was inducement enow' to tak' the King's shilling."

Since her mother's displeasure was obvious, it was tactless of Louisa Brome to interrupt her.

"But, Mama, they're *our* Highlanders too! You cannot have forgotten how Charlotte and Susan and Madelina and I—and even wee Georgy—danced at the market at Tomintoul with any young man willing to wear King George's cockade."

"Aye, I mind it well enow. What a charming picture you all made in your tartan petticoats and pantaloons, with your tartan scarves and Highland bonnets wi' the cocks' feathers—your papa being the Cock o' the North. But that still doesna' make the Gordon Highlanders *your* regiment." Clearly the duchess was by no means mollified. "And who gave a new tartan to the Gordons? Your mama!

I took the Black Watch plaid and into it I had woven a yellow thread, as well we all ken."

The duchess's daughters exchanged glances and settled themselves more comfortably in their seats as Charlotte whispered to Louisa, "You shouldn't have teased Mama. Now she's going to tell us the whole story all over again, and we shall be here forever."

Charlotte's foreboding was correct, because this story was one the Duchess of Gordon never tired of telling.

"Ye'll mind—except Georgy, who was only a bairn— that in 1792 the Princesse de Lamballe, the great friend of puir Queen Marie Antoinette, was sent by her to England on a secret mission. By then the king and queen were prisoners of those bluidy *sans-culottes* and desperate for any help to rescue them—that was why they looked to England, even though the French and the English have always been enemies, but not, of course, the French and the Scots. Between us there was always the Auld Alliance ever since the days of Mary, Queen of Scots, God rest her puir soul."

The duchess was now on the flood tide of her tale.

"The princess sought me out as being the most powerful woman in England and the one who had the ear of Mr. Pitt. What she wanted from him was a promise that the British would make war on the French and release the king and queen of France from their jailers. I was very ready to oblige the princess, but for once Mr. Pitt would not oblige me.

" 'I canna' mak' war on France at this moment, Duchess,' he told me. 'For the time being it serves our interests best to remain neutral.' "

Jane Gordon heaved a sigh.

"So the puir Princesse de Lamballe went back to France with her tail all raggle-taggle between her legs, and the next thing we knew was that the king and queen were taken from their palace of the Tuileries, and the princess along with them."

Since her daughters knew what was coming next, the effect of the duchess's dramatic pause was lost on them.

"Then came the bluidy massacres—September massacres, they were called—and the mob seized the princess, murdered her, mutilated her body, and then cut off her head."

Georgiana's hands were already over her ears, so the duchess said tolerantly, "On account of Georgy's squeamishness, I'll spare you the details, but they were obscene —obscene," she repeated with relish. "But what I will tell you is that when those filthy murderers had cut off the puir woman's head, they took it to a wretched hairdresser and forced him to dress her hair—and a fine head of hair she had, long and very fair. Then they put the bleeding head on a pike and paraded it under the windows of the Temple prison, calling the Queen with foul jests to come and bid farewell to her friend."

At this point in Jane Gordon's story, her two duchess daughters and Lady Brome, knowing their cue, shuddered for their mother's benefit.

"That was too much! When the news of the puir creature's murder and the insults to her corpse reached England, I rushed to Downing Street, and there I stayed with Mr. Pitt until I convinced him that as long as those murdering savages of *sans-culottes* were abroad in the world, it would be a disgrace to these islands.

" 'But, Duchess,' William Pitt objected, 'we canna' mak' war without soldiers.'

"And that I didna' need Mr. Pitt to tell me!

" 'If we go to war, we must have men,' he repeated. 'We must raise new regiments. The Duke of Gordon has already done yeoman service by raising regiments of Fencibles, and His Majesty's government is grateful for his

"Ye're no' grateful enough, Georgiana," she complained, "for the sacrifices I make for ye. Ye ken that I stayed the whole evening in the ballroom only for your sake."

"You are mistaken, Mama. I do indeed know how kind you are."

What Georgiana really knew was that the duchess's ill humor was due to her having been obliged to forgo her cherished game of hazard, and that she was still smarting because Charlotte had produced the season's greatest novelty. Now, until winter brought everyone back to town, the duchess would have no opportunity of going one better than her daughter. While her ill temper persisted, it was useless for Georgiana to question her, because a vague answer would be all that she would get.

She would have been astonished to know that a few hundred yards away from Pall Mall, at the Duke of Bedford's house in Arlington Street, Lord John Russell was subjecting his brother to the interrogation to which Georgiana would have liked to submit her mother.

"But, Francis, I cannot understand your hesitation. She's an absolutely charming girl, so full of gaiety and high spirits, and as pretty as a picture. You could not do better. She'd bring some life into old Woburn Abbey."

"You think so?" asked the duke indifferently, paying less attention to his brother's words than to fondling the ears of the spaniel lying at his feet. "So you want to deliver me bound hand and foot into the clutches of the Matchmaking Duchess? Why should I be the next victim of her duchess-mania—and anyway the girl—what's the chit's name, Georgiana?—is not in the least interested in pigs."

John shook his brother's shoulder affectionately.

"*Touché!* I'm willing to grant you everything you say about the duchess, but it is a mistake to underestimate her. The Duchess of Gordon is a power in the land, far

greater than Georgiana Devonshire. Personally, in spite
of her shocking language and highhanded ways, at times
I cannot help but like her—she has so much vitality,
and a rare sense of humor."

"But you are not suggesting that I marry Jane Gordon," Bedford broke in.

"No, of course not!" John was impatient. "But I
hope you will seriously consider marrying her daughter.
You are an old stick-in-the-mud, Francis. Just because
you think of nothing but sheep and pigs is no reason why
a pretty young girl should share your interest in them.
Anyway, there's quite enough for a Duchess of Bedford
to do at Woburn and in Devonshire and Newton Stewart
without her having to take an interest in piggeries and
cowsheds."

Francis sighed and absent-mindedly tweaked his
spaniel's ears, provoking a sharp yelp from his pet.

"My dear brother, if only to silence you, I will pay a
formal call on the duchess and invite her to the sheep-
shearing, but don't think the prospect fills me with any
pleasure. Good Lord, to have Jane Gordon nagging at me
for a week about her precious William Pitt! In fact, if it
gratifies you to hear it, I said as much to the girl—
about inviting her and her mother, I mean—and then,
chè sarà sarà."

With that John Russell had to be content, because his
brother refused to say another word. It was a victory of
sorts for him. He simply could not understand Francis's
reluctance. Had his own marriage to Georgiana Gordon
been in question, he knew he would have needed no second bidding—she really was a most captivating girl. It was
not only her beauty, he mused, which made her so
appealing, but a sunniness, so different from . . . He stifled
the disloyal thought which had risen unprompted to his
mind to concentrate on ways of bringing Francis around.

John did most truly believe that Georgiana was the right wife for him—if only his brother could be made to realize his luck.

All through the sheep-shearing week, however, Francis seemed indifferent to anything but the constant activity in sheepfolds and byres, and was more often found in breeches and leggings than in the formal dress of a host.

Jane Gordon was almost at her wits' end when she saw that the duke had made no move toward Georgiana, but she had an unsuspected ally in John Russell. He had observed the malicious smiles cast by some of the guests, and overheard the tittering whispers.

"I'll lay a hundred guineas that the Duchess of Gordon is about to forfeit her title of the Matchmaking Duchess. Did not a little bird tell me that she came to Woburn expecting Bedford to declare himself?"

"I'm not taking you. It's plain enough that he's slipping out of her clutches, and what will Mother Gordon do then? Not another bachelor duke in the country."

Seeing John, the speakers had stopped abruptly and drifted away in embarrassment, but they had sufficiently aroused his pique. He was not going to stand idly by and see that delightful girl, Georgiana Gordon, made an object of the world's ridicule. He sought out his brother and asked him bluntly, "Francis, do you or do you not intend to offer for Georgiana Gordon? I understood that you had made up your mind to do so. Why, then, are you shilly-shallying?"

The duke looked pensive. John rarely spoke to him so sternly or with such intent, but Francis intended to keep secret, even from his much loved brother that, all through this week, his indifference to Georgiana had been more apparent than real. He had, in fact, been watching her closely, and in spite of his determination not to be drawn in, he had been attracted by her freshness and gaiety.

"Do not agitate yourself, I beg, John," the duke yawned, "and do not harass me. It is on the cards that I shall oblige you."

John bit back an angry retort. Francis would not have given even so halfhearted a promise if he had not intended to abide by it, but it was intolerable that he should treat the prospect of marriage to Georgiana Gordon so cavalierly. John left the room brusquely while Francis pondered, "What can be the matter with the old fellow? After all, I have yielded to his wishes. I suppose that dreary wife of his has been nagging at him again."

A moment later he had dismissed John's peculiar behavior from his mind as he became immersed in Coke of Norfolk's theories on the breeding of sheep—a topic which he found far more to his taste than the breeding of heirs.

John did not find it so easy to slough off his anger and distress. Indeed, so enraged was he with his brother that even when he met Georgiana in the corridor, he had no more than a curt nod for her, which left her astonished and troubled. What could she have said or done to make him so short with her? She had left her room in the secret hope of meeting John, and now she found herself at a loss. Her mother was still abed, having sat up till the small hours playing hazard.

Georgiana stepped out through the long windows of the Venetian Room and stood for a moment, looking at but not seeing the roses in the small garden. Her thoughts were focused on John's curious coldness. Suddenly, she heard behind her the unwelcome sound of the duke's voice. Chancing to look up from his treatise, he had seen Georgiana through the library windows, standing alone, and decided that this moment was as good as any to put a halter around his neck.

"I am glad to have found you alone for once, ma'am,"

he said suavely. "Indeed, I owe you many apologies for having been so poor a host during your stay at Woburn, but I have no doubt that my brother proved an excellent substitute."

To agree that John had indeed proved himself more than a substitute would have been impolite, and Georgiana merely gave a tight little smile.

"Are you perhaps about to take a walk? May I have the pleasure of accompanying you? Is there some spot you would especially like to visit, the Shell Room, the Grotto, or the Sculpture Room? I am yours to command."

It was on the tip of Georgiana's tongue to ask to be shown the piggeries, but she caught herself in time. If the duke's extraordinary civility and his object in seeking her out was to make her an offer, then, so far as she was concerned, the piggeries were as good a place as any other in which to make it—perhaps the most appropriate! However little romance there was to be found among pigs, for Georgiana Gordon there could not be less in a proposal from the Duke of Bedford!

Since the duchess had decided willy-nilly that Georgiana should marry him, there seemed little point in trying to postpone the moment she so much dreaded.

"Your brother has most kindly shown me all those places, Duke." She heard a mechanical voice speaking which was scarcely recognizable as her own. "But perhaps we might revisit the Chinese dairy, which I find charming."

"I am delighted that you do, ma'am. I built it specially to house my collection of Chinese porcelain."

As if anxious to atone for his previous lapses in courtesy, the duke now showed himself very attentive.

"May I procure you a parasol, Lady Georgiana? The sun is very hot for June."

Georgiana declined, still with the sensation that the

voice issuing from her mouth was not her own. Procuring a parasol would entail further delay, and she was anxious that this painful interview be over and done with as soon as possible. She and her escort exchanged only the most superficial commonplaces as they strolled across the Abbey lawns under the great cedar, leaving the massive stable block on their right. All at once, with Georgiana beside him, Francis became aware, as Jane Gordon had hoped, of the contrast between the aging, worn Nancy Maynard and this girl, so young, so fresh, and, yes, so desirable. Georgiana, he was comfortably confident, was his for the asking.

As Georgiana knelt down by the little lake to ring the bells which summoned the fish to come to take their food, once again she heard behind her the duke's voice, but with a new note in it, which made her panic.

"Lady Georgiana, will you do me the honor of bestowing on me your hand in marriage?"

In her agitation, Georgiana almost fell forward into the lake. As she drew herself back, she wished that she could have fallen into watery oblivion, and longed to throw the duke's formal, stilted words back into his teeth. She wanted to tell him that nothing would persuade her to marry him, that she had taken an incurable dislike to him, but the lump in her throat prevented her uttering a syllable, nor did she dare do so. Desolately she bowed her head, more in deference to her mother's wishes than in acceptance of the duke's offer.

As he possessed himself of Georgiana's hand, wet from trailing in the lake, and planted a kiss on it, Francis experienced an unexpected pleasure. The feel of her soft, sweet flesh roused him to seize her in his arms and embrace her with a passion which disgusted and frightened her. After a declaration so icy and lacking in any sign of affection, she had not looked for any ardor. She tore herself free and stumbled away.

Francis made no move to follow her but, with a faint smile on his lips, remained standing by the lake before turning in to the Chinese dairy. The future promised to be both interesting and titillating. Decidedly, Georgiana would be an admirable exchange for Nancy. She was, of course, a silly little goose, but he had no doubts of her growing up once they were married. Should he gratify old John by telling him that he had been right?

John himself was striding savagely from the woods toward the house when he encountered Georgiana, who was half walking, half running back to the Abbey.

"Lady Georgy, is anything amiss? You are distressed! Can I be of any service to you?"

"No—yes—no—there is nothing amiss, only . . . only . . . your brother has made me an offer of marriage, which I have accepted."

As Georgiana ran on into the house, winking away her tears, John made no effort to detain her. Only now that the blow had fallen did he begin to understand the true nature of his feelings, and then he wondered about Georgiana's. Was her distress merely the normal reaction of a girl who had just received an offer of marriage, or was it that she did not care for Francis? In any event, he told himself wearily that it could be no concern of his.

"Mama, the duke has made me his offer, and I have accepted it. I hope you are happy, because I am not!"

The tears which Georgiana had been holding at bay now fell unchecked as the duchess, clucking her joy, folded her weeping daughter in her arms.

"My darling Georgy, you have indeed made me happy, and of course you're happy yourself—you just do not realize it yet. Dinna' fret, my bairnie, it's just the shock that ye are to be a duchess. Think, Georgy, I shall have five daughters married, and four of them to dukes! Dinna' contradict me now, Georgy—och, if only puir Madelina hadna' been so headstrong!"

Passionately Georgiana wished that she had half Madelina's strength of character, but she found it impossible to withstand the duchess's will. Coldly she disengaged herself from her mother's embrace and unwelcome jubilation to let her tears have full reign. The duchess, with unusual restraint, made no attempt to stop her, but she muttered savagely to herself, "I'll wager that fool Bedford went all the wrong way about it. But what can you expect of a man who's spent his life consorting with drabs out of stews and pigs in sties—and a Whig to boot! He ought to have known that whatever her mother has done, she's seen to it that Georgiana is as innocent as a dove."

Briefly the thought crossed the duchess's mind that perhaps it might have been better for her daughter if some penniless young man had already crossed her path, but she dismissed it quickly, to console herself that before the marriage took place she would give Bedford—and Georgiana—some useful advice. A little innocence did not hurt men, but they could have too much of it.

Before the Gordon ladies left Woburn the next day, Jane Gordon settled with the duke that the wedding should take place in four months' time, in October.

"You appreciate, ma'am," said Francis significantly, "that I must make some changes in my household here."

The duchess nodded assent with a stately air and an inward chuckle as she pictured his forthcoming scene with Nancy Maynard. When he told her to shake the dust of Woburn Abbey off her feet forever, she would undoubtedly fly into a rage.

"I understand you perfectly, Duke, and naturally the

preparations for the wedding cannot be hurried. My experience in the matter is large, as you know, but after all, it is not every day that a duke marries a duke's daughter."

Fortunately, Georgiana was not present to hear her mother's boast.

"No doubt, ma'am, you will also wish to obtain the duke's consent to the marriage."

The duchess looked puzzled for a moment before she exclaimed, "Och, you mean my husband? Dinna' worry about Alexander. The Duke of Gordon will do what the Duchess of Gordon tells him to do."

Francis gave a wry smile to the formidable mother-in-law he had chosen.

"Then, ma'am, I will send a notice to the *Gazette*, and I shall look forward to having the pleasure of calling on you and Lady Georgiana soon in town."

To Georgiana's relief, the duke's farewell of her was purely formal, and, with youthful optimism, she hoped desperately that something somehow might arise which would prevent her from ever seeing him or Woburn Abbey again.

On their return to London, dozens of congratulatory wishes, which were hard for Georgiana to endure, poured into Buckingham House. Only in Damour did she find a sympathizer, but his sympathy had perforce to be mute. It was expressed only by looks and prompt attention to her wishes.

The duchess, plunging into a joyous orgy of shopping, was for the most part too happily engaged to observe that Georgiana was listless and unenthusiastic beside her. When she did at last notice, she scolded her daughter.

"Georgy, I cannot think why you have lost your spirits. Any other girl would be delirious with joy."

"But I am not any other girl, Mama. I am Georgiana

Gordon, and you know, if only you would not set yourself against knowing, that I have not the faintest wish to marry the Duke of Bedford. I am going to do so only because it is *your* wish, but do not expect me to rejoice in my betrothal."

Thereafter, even in the face of her mother's displeasure Georgiana maintained a withdrawn silence, until finally the duchess washed her hands of her and continued her preparations for the wedding in the company of one or another of her married daughters.

On her return one day, quite worn out from her exertions, the duchess was pleased to find Georgiana looking much brighter as she eagerly held out a letter for her mother to read.

"Mama, this letter is from the duke. He writes that Lady John Russell has died—surely that means the wedding must be postponed?"

"Goddamn Georgiana Russell," swore the duchess as she snatched the letter. "If ever there were a foolish, inconsiderate woman! Bedford is so set on doing the correct thing that he will certainly not consider marrying while his brother is in deep mourning—or at least for six months. That means the wedding cannot take place until April, and no doubt all the fashions will have changed by then. Oh, damn and blast Georgiana Russell!"

"Perhaps it also means that the wedding will never take place, Mama," was Georgiana's quiet rejoinder.

The duchess turned sharply to vent all her pent-up irritation on her daughter.

"Georgiana Gordon! Dinna' ye dare say anything so wicked! You'll marry the Duke of Bedford and be his duchess if it's the last thing on earth I contrive!"

Chapter Three

"Because you've taken a fancy to a younger face, I have to go! I cannot believe you to be serious, Francis!"

Nancy Maynard and Francis Bedford faced each other in the library at Woburn Abbey. The duke lounged in an armchair and coolly watched his mistress pace up and down the long room.

"You flatter yourself," she spat at him, "that you'll get an heir on her, but I doubt if you're capable of it! If you were, I'd have had a child in all these years we've been together. But I haven't, have I?"

In spite of his apparent indifference, Francis winced at the taunt.

"Don't be vulgar, Nancy! It does not become you."

With distaste the duke registered how the red which flushed Nancy's face and neck turned her into an ugly woman. All the lotions and unguents she used to preserve her beauty could not prevent her in her rages from looking like a scraggy old hen. It was on the tip of Francis's tongue to tell her so, but he refrained. He had no wish to descend to her level of abuse.

"Oh, so I'm vulgar now!" Nancy stormed. "But, may I remind you, there have been times when you liked my vulgarity very well. And I suppose your future mother-in-law's not vulgar, oh no! Her language comes straight from the farmyard! The great aristocrat, the moralizing Duchess of Gordon, draws her skirts away from the Viscountess Maynard and shelters her namby-pamby daughter from contamination by the Duke of Bedford's light o' love. Everyone knows Jane Gordon hasn't a moral bone in her body and boasts all over London that her husband never fathered her daughters. A fine lady forsooth! And to make room for her bastard, I've got to move out of Woburn Abbey!"

Francis looked coldly at Nancy.

"Ah, so at last we get the truth. It's not me but the comfort and luxury of the Abbey you regret losing. I must say, you've deceived me very prettily all these years but, storm and rage as you will, Nancy, you'll leave Woburn within the sennight—*and* you'll make no more scenes before you go!"

The duke rose languidly from his chair and strolled toward the door. He paused and turned to say, "Of course, I'll provide suitably for you, and I should like to thank you for the pleasure you have given me in the past. I do not deny that our association has been a comfortable one for us both. Do not spoil the memory of it now."

Francis bowed, but Nancy clawed at his arm, preventing his leaving the room.

"Getting sentimental, Francis," she jeered. "You can afford to do so when you're casting me off like an old shoe. No doubt you don't think I'll go to see your innocent little Georgiana and tell her what you've been to me.

Innocent! I'll wager she's no innocent. Wait till you've married her and she plays you the same tricks her mother played on *her* duke!"

Nancy's voice broke on a sob, but it was a sob of rage.

"Don't pretend to cry, Nancy." The duke's voice was icy. "You're no actress and you never were. Your career was made in a bagnio."

"That's a lie," Nancy shrieked. "I was respectably born in Bond Street and I was married to Edward Horton—and he was a gentleman, which is more than can be said for you! It wasn't my fault he left me penniless and I was obliged to accept the protection of the Duke of Grafton. After all, he was Prime Minister, so that it was practically his duty to take care of me."

"Come, come, Nancy." The Duke of Bedford raised an eyebrow. "And what about all the others, and the Duke of Dorset! I'll say this for you, you've always flown high, but it's over now, at least so far as one duke is concerned! If you were a sportsman you'd know how to take a toss."

"And you've taken plenty of tosses in my bed," Nancy thrust venomously at him.

"That's enough! Do not bring the language of Gin Lane into Woburn Abbey, if you please. I am going to town tomorrow, and on my return I do not expect to find you here. There are other dukes, you know, and I have no doubt that you will contrive to establish yourself in the luxury to which I have accustomed you, but you may not remain longer at Woburn. That is my last word."

The duke shook off Nancy's restraining arm and quitted the library, leaving behind him an angry and frustrated woman. Nancy knew her threats were idle and that an interview with Lady Georgiana would avail her nothing because if the Duchess of Gordon were determined that her daughter marry the Duke of Bedford, she would care not a fig if he had kept a harem of women at Woburn or elsewhere. Nancy looked around the room balefully, deciding which valuable objects she could remove without their being immediately missed. This resolve cheered her up a little, and she went thoughtfully to her own room, on the first floor next to the empty nurseries.

To his surprise, Francis was more shaken than he had expected at parting from Nancy. She was a habit of long standing and of all his mistresses she had suited him best, but today's scene only confirmed what he already knew—she was past her prime, while Georgiana Gordon was young and delectable. He was equally as indifferent to Nancy's gibes about Jane Gordon's marital fidelity as to those about the Duke of Gordon's illegitimate family. Nancy knew the way of the world. Provided you gave your husband an heir of his own body, society turned a blind eye to the question of who fathered your other children. Nevertheless, he was thankful that he himself did not have a brood of bastards, and he would make very sure that any children born of his marriage to Georgiana would be Russells by parentage as well as by name.

It was unfortunate that the marriage must be postponed for six months, but the duchess was correct in thinking that Francis's rigid sense of propriety in some things would not allow him to agree even to a quiet and simple ceremony during the period of deep mourning for his sister-in-law.

The duchess alternated her lamentations at the delay with oaths directed at Georgiana Russell's lack of consideration in dying when she did. Having succeeded in catching the most eligible prize in England for her daughter she had determined that nothing would stand in the way of realizing her ambition to make Georgiana's wedding the most splendid of the century.

"Such a grand wedding I planned for you—the bonny

bride you will make," she mourned, but she met with little sympathy from Georgiana.

"Mama," she asked nervously, as for the hundredth time the duchess gloated on all the details of the ceremony to take place the following April, "I hope I shan't be obliged to do all those things which Susan did at her wedding— like tying a bread creel on Manchester's back and cutting the cords to show that a wife eases her husband's burden? I'm sure I shan't ease Bedford's burdens, however many he has, and for another thing, I don't want to! And I hope no one's going to throw a glass of whisky in my face to have it running all down my gown."

"Och, Georgy, don't be silly! These things are only done at a Scottish wedding, and *you* won't be married like your sister at Gordon Castle, however much your Papa might want it. Who's going to travel up to Aberdeen in the middle of the season? Not Mr. Pitt, I'll be bound, and I'd as soon you didn't marry at all as not have the Prime Minister at your wedding!"

Georgiana made a face. The one person she wished would not be at her wedding was herself!

"He's not the Prime Minister, anyway . . ."

"Don't interrupt! If he's resigned it won't be for long, and he'll be back in office any day now. No," the duchess continued briskly. "You'll be married at St. George's, Hanover Square, and the wedding breakfast will be here at Buckingham House—Damour and I have arranged it all. Nothing like it will ever have been seen before, so many soups, roasts, entrées, removes, and a great *pièce montée* of sugar work with the Russell and Gordon arms entwined! Now, what do you think of that, Georgy? You couldn't have anything like that in Scotland. And you won't be bedded by the guests, either," added the duchess as a regretful afterthought.

Georgiana turned her head away. Why did Mama insist

on dwelling on something about which she herself did not care to think? To divert the duchess's mind from this unwelcome prospect, she asked quickly, "But Papa *will* give me away, won't he?"

"I suppose so" was the gloomy answer, "now that the wedding's to be in April. In October he wouldn't come to town on account of the pheasants, but in April he'll be at a loss with nothing to shoot."

At once Georgiana felt the need to protest on her father's behalf.

"Papa wrote me a very civil letter of congratulations, Mama. I should like him to be at the wedding and to give me away."

"You'll probably get your wish, Georgy. He knows what's expected of him. However, there's no need to meet trouble halfway. We've a few months of peace before he's likely to come down to London."

These months passed all too quickly for Georgiana, who at times was at screaming point as the duchess paraded her triumph to the *ton*. She had hoped against hope that something would occur to prevent her wedding, but as April drew nearer any expectation of a reprieve faded, and her spirits sank ever deeper.

"I do wish, Georgy," moaned the duchess, "that you would show a little more consideration for all my exertions on your behalf. I declare, I feel just like Polly Peachum's father in *The Beggar's Opera*, which we saw last night —'Tis wonder any man alive would ever rear a daughter!' Not, of course, that anyone would compare the Duke of Bedford with a highwayman like Captain Macheath."

"We had far better have gone to see *The Mourning Bride*," retorted Georgiana. "Please understand, Mama, that what you are making me do is for your own sake— it is *you* who want me to marry the duke in order to have another duchess in your family, but you know very well that *I* have no wish to marry him."

"Stuff and nonsense, Georgiana Gordon! You irritate me past bearing. Where, I ask you, will you find anyone more elegant in his person or polished in his manners than Francis Bedford?"

"That's just it, Mama! He's so polished, one cannot even scratch that hard, brilliant surface."

In fact, Georgiana, remembering the duke's passionate embrace, knew what roughness lay underneath the polished exterior, but she had not spoken of it to her mother then, nor did she wish to do so now. It was true that Francis treated his future bride with distant courtesy on his rare visits to London, but he promised himself to make up for his restraint after the wedding. Georgiana in her turn was chillingly polite, hoping in desperation that Francis would find her so insipid that he would cry off. She was unaware of the fact that the more she retreated, the more she stimulated his ardor, and that nothing was further from his thoughts than to break the engagement.

Francis made his excuses to the duchess for failing to visit her and her daughter as often as he wished.

"I have reached an impasse, ma'am, in a vital agricultural experiment, and it is essential that I remain at Woburn to watch its progress or all my work will go for nothing."

The duchess scarcely needed even this veiled hint to realize that the impasse he had reached had no connection with agriculture but with his difficulty in getting Nancy to leave Woburn. He was extremely angry to find her still in residence when he returned to the Abbey at the end of the week.

"I don't care a farthing that you want me to go," Nancy stormed at him. "Here I am and here I stay—and what will you do about it?"

"What I shall do, Nancy," the duke answered with icy sternness, "is to have you carried out of the house by my footmen. I cannot believe that you would choose that undignified way of leaving, but if you will not go of your own free will, I promise you that is the way you *will* go."

Convinced now that anger would avail her nothing, Nancy tried to arouse Francis's pity. She stretched out her arms to him, sobbing, "You cannot do this to me, Francis, after all we've been to each other!"

"I can and I will, Nancy. Pack your bags and get you gone."

Francis cast a quick look around the library.

"And I should be obliged if you would restore those objects which have unaccountably disappeared since I last entered this room. I told you that I would provide suitably for you, but that did not mean you were to despoil Woburn Abbey!"

Nancy dropped her arms to glare balefully at Francis; then she flounced out of the library, banging the door behind her. Francis sank into a chair. Nancy's scenes always gave him an infernal headache.

When Francis paid a brief visit to town early in February, the Duchess of Gordon noted with alarm his great lack of spirit, and he confessed to her that he was feeling far from well.

"You know, ma'am, when I was a boy at Westminster School I was hit by a cricket ball, and from time to time I still feel the effects here."

Francis touched his right side.

"I trust, Duke, that it is no more than a passing malaise. It would be unfortunate indeed if there were to be a further postponement of the wedding."

"Rest assured, ma'am, that nothing shall again be allowed to interfere with the wedding. You may believe me when I tell you that, with the passing of each day, my impatience and my eagerness increase."

The duchess glowed, but Georgiana, with a marked show of indifference, did not lift her head from the tapestry she was working.

"You refuse to listen to me, Georgiana," the duchess scolded after Francis had taken his departure, "when I tell you that he has a great regard for you, and whatever *you* may think, he's showing it by every means in his power. Before you came into the room, he told me that at last he's rid himself of that common creature, Nancy Parsons. Oh, don't open your eyes so wide at me! You know very well that she's Francis's mistress, and has been for years. I really canna' understand how any daughter of mine can be so ignorant."

Georgiana disdained to reply, and the duchess had to continue her scolding with no response from her daughter.

Jane Gordon was distracted from perpetually harping on the wedding by a fresh interest: the peace negotiations with France, which were proceeding at Amiens. Now her constant refrain was "Think, Georgy, after ten years of war, we're at last going to make peace, and all thanks to Mr. Pitt. When Austria made peace with France last year, I thought it couldna' be long before we did the same. Is it not fortunate that Louisa's father-in-law should be our chief delegate to the peace talks? How wise I was to marry her to Brome, because there can be no doubt of Lord Cornwallis being made duke if the negotiations are successful."

"If anyone heard you, Mama," said Georgiana sourly, unable to banish the disloyal thought that her mother's insistence on dukes smacked more of the parvenu than of the established nobility, "they would think our making peace with France was fortunate solely because another of your daughters might become a duchess."

"Don't be absurd, Georgiana. As if I could ever rate my own above the country's interest! I cannot help thinking, though, that if peace is made, you will be able to go to Paris for your honeymoon. Is that not an inviting prospect?"

"Not to me! It isn't where you go for your honeymoon that matters—it's with whom you go."

Was that dratted girl never going to come out of the sulks? Her willfulness was wearing the duchess out. In another minute she was really going to lose her temper.

"I am going to walk over to Louisa's house to see if she has heard anything further from Cornwallis. I am sure he lets Brome know what is happening. You may come with me if you wish, Georgiana."

Anything was better than being cooped up alone with her mother, Georgiana felt, as she went to put on her bonnet and pelisse to walk the short distance from Pall Mall to her sister's house in York Street.

As the weeks went by, she became increasingly weary of the duchess's new obsession.

"What a pity," exclaimed the duchess one day when she returned home from one of her lengthy sojourns in the gallery of the House of Commons, "that Francis is a Whig. His support in the Lords would be most valuable to dear Mr. Pitt. When you are married perhaps you will be able to persuade him to change his allegiance, Georgy."

Georgiana forbore to say it was highly unlikely that so staunch a Whig as the Duke of Bedford would change his political opinions merely to oblige his mother-in-law.

"Your Grace, here is an express just come for you from Woburn," announced Damour one afternoon late in February.

Eagerly the duchess broke the seal and rapidly scanned the letter. It was brief and said merely that the duke had been slightly indisposed for a few days with a cold.

As he was coughing badly, it would be wisest, he considered, to postpone his visit to town. In his place his attorney, Mr. Grimes, would wait on the duchess at her convenience.

"Francis has a cold and cannot come to town," the duchess informed Georgiana, who showed an obvious indifference to the duke's letter. "He is sending his attorney to conclude the settlements with me, as leaving them to your Papa would be quite useless. He would be sure to stipulate only that you had enough horses and hounds at your disposal; I doubt if he would give so much as a thought to your pin money or your jointure. As usual, everything falls on me!"

Quite obviously, the duchess's words hid her real satisfaction at holding everything securely in her own hands. Had the Duke of Gordon even expressed a wish to negotiate his daughter's marriage settlements, his wife would not have tolerated his interference.

While the duchess was happily employed calculating Georgiana's widow's jointure and deciding that five thousand pounds a year would be insufficient for her to keep up the state of a dowager duchess, she was interrupted by yet another express from Woburn. Even Georgiana's curiosity was aroused as she saw a look of dismay deepen on her mother's face.

"Georgy, this letter is from Lord John. He says the duke's condition has worsened. It is a recurrence of his old trouble, that damned cricket ball—men and their sports! He is in great pain, it seems. All the remedies they have tried have proved useless, and Lord John says that Francis's surgeon has been sent for, as an operation may be required."

Georgiana was far too tender-hearted not to be sorry for anyone suffering pain but, as she murmured a few formal words of regret, her spirits rose a little in spite of herself. If Francis were to be ill for any length of time, the wedding might again have to be postponed. She was careful, of course, to voice nothing of this hope and call down on her head the duchess's wrath. In any case, her mother was paying her no attention but was bustling about, summoning one servant after another.

"Damour, Damour, have my traveling carriage made ready. I am posting immediately to Woburn. And send my woman to me. I must take my night clothes, because I shall be obliged to stay the night at least."

"You don't want me to go with you, Mama?" Georgiana asked fearfully.

"No, no, Georgy, a sickroom is no place for you. I know how much you long to see Francis, and so you shall, once he is better, but now you must be patient and stay at home."

Georgiana was forced to smile because, in spite of all her protests, the duchess obstinately refused to recognize that her daughter was not passionately devoted to her betrothed. When Jane Gordon was finally installed in her carriage and her horses' heads were turned to the north, Georgiana heaved a great sigh of relief at the unwonted luxury of finding herself alone.

The road to Woburn was choked with carriages sent from town to make civil inquiries after the duke's health, but the scarcity of post horses available did not trouble the Duchess of Gordon. She simply commandeered the duke's own horses, stabled along the Great North Road as relays for the despatch of expresses to London.

The duchess was shown into the Venetian Room while Lord John Russell was informed of her arrival. She looked into the ante-library and the library, but they were empty, except for the pall of gloom which hung over the whole Abbey and alarmed her greatly. Her alarm increased when at last Lord John hurried into the Venetian Room, wearing an expression of great anxiety.

"You will forgive me, ma'am, if I am able to spare you only a moment, as I am in constant attendance on my brother. Although his sufferings are, alas, very great, he is bearing them with unexampled submission and fortitude."

In answer to the duchess's nervous question, Lord John replied slowly, "Yes, the surgeons have operated on him. Under the excruciating pain of the knife he made no more than a groan or two. His courage was remarkable."

For a moment Lord John turned his head away. When he continued after a momentary silence it was plain that he was controlling his emotion and the anguish he felt over his brother's condition.

"I must return to him, ma'am, as you will understand. Our people will see to your needs—I will send the major-domo to attend to your wishes. It was indeed good of you to come. I trust Lady Georgiana is not too overset by this sad news."

John banished the thought that Jane Gordon's visit was officious. All his thoughts were focused on his brother, and he concentrated all his energies on aiding his recovery. With a hurried bow, he left the duchess to return to the duke's bedroom, where Francis, his face drawn with pain, was propped up on pillows. As John approached the bedside, Francis managed a small smile.

"I have made the final arrangements for the disposal of my property," he murmured in a faint voice. "It all comes to you, John. I know you will carry on the work which I have begun, and will be very successful at it. I have left you a letter which you will read when I am gone."

"Nonsense, Francis, do not speak of leaving us! Of course you will get better."

"No, old fellow . . ."

Feebly Francis extended his hand, which John grasped in warm affection, as he tried to inject his own life force into his brother. Francis gave him a grateful glance before turning his head on the pillow with a gentle sigh. Silence fell until the surgeon stepped forward and said quietly, "His Grace has left us, Your Grace."

At the unfamiliar address, John started and put out his hand as if to push the thought away. Good God, could they not even let Francis breathe his last before they began toadying to his brother? Tenderly he closed his brother's eyes and suffered himself to be led from the room, too overcome with grief for any other feeling. Two bereavements in so short a space of time—but he knew which affected him most deeply!

News of the duke's death was conveyed to the Duchess of Gordon, together with John's apologies for not informing her in person.

"His Grace is sure that you will understand that at this moment he does not feel able to see anyone," said Mr. Grimes.

The duchess bowed in a most stately manner.

"Kindly transmit my deep condolences to His Grace. I will write to him personally when I return to town."

The hatchments were already being nailed up over the door as the Duchess of Gordon drove away from Woburn Abbey. Her woman was the only person to hear her loud and indiscreet lamentations.

Immediately on her return to Buckingham House she sought out Georgiana and took her daughter in her arms.

"My puir, wee bairnie, Francis is no more! He died this morning, and my darling Georgy is a widow!"

"Scarcely a widow, Mama, before being a wife!"

No sooner were the words out of her mouth than Georgiana was ashamed of having spoken so tartly but her grief for the duke was no greater than it would have been for any other gentleman of her acquaintance.

"Why, if he had to die, could Francis not have died a month later," wailed the duchess, wringing her hands. "He should have tried to live at least until after the wedding. It was his duty to do so. You would have been a dowager duchess—so touching to be a dowager duchess at the age of twenty."

"You are mistaken, Mama, not a dowager duchess—there is no Duchess of Bedford now."

"I forgot that. Of course, Lord John is a widower. Damn that Georgiana Russell, she started it all—just what one might have expected of her, the disobliging creature."

Georgiana was thankful that hers were the only ears to hear her mother's unseemly railing. She herself was still too bewildered by her sudden release to realize that now she would not be obliged to marry the Duke of Bedford. This would take time and a relaxation of the tensions of the past few months, if only her mother would give her peace enough to recover. Georgiana's heart sank when the duchess suddenly interrupted her complaints to clap her hands in excitement. What preposterous idea was she now going to put forward? Her worst fears were fulfilled when the duchess exclaimed energetically, "You must go into mourning, my love. I would wish you to show every sign of respect to Francis," Jane Gordon continued. "After all, it is a feather in a girl's cap to have been intended for the Duke of Bedford, even if he was so lacking in consideration as to die before the wedding. With your fair coloring you will look ravishing in black—the mourning bride indeed. How fortunate that you should have mentioned the play."

Georgiana looked incredulous, but the duchess ignored her, wholly absorbed as she was in her plan. She bustled away, greatly delighted, to order black clothes for Georgiana and black ribbons for herself. How pathetic darling Georgy would look, and the world at large could not fail to regard her as other than the widowed Duchess of Bedford. Yes, it was a splendid idea, but was it enough? There must be something else she could do, something even more spectacular than putting Georgiana into mourning to impress the *ton*.

Jane Gordon gave a sudden crow of triumph. She and Georgiana would attend the duke's funeral. That it was not customary for women to do so mattered to her not a whit. All her life the Duchess of Gordon had flouted convention.

Georgiana was horrified when told that she was to accompany her mother to the little family church at Chenies in Buckinghamshire, where the fifth Duke of Bedford was to be laid to rest among so many of his forebears.

"You cannot mean to go, Mama! It would be putting ourselves forward in a most detestable way. I am sure it will create a most terrible scandal."

"Rubbish, Georgiana. If I say we are going to the funeral, we are going. And when did Jane Gordon ever care for what the world says? Indeed, all the world will say is that you are showing an exceptional mark of devotion to your betrothed."

Further protest was useless once the bit was well and truly between the duchess's teeth.

"I fear, Georgy," the duchess said regretfully, "that we must go directly to Chenies, since the funeral procession will travel through the night and it will be too exhausting. We must, however, arrive in good time to follow the coffin into the church."

But when the Gordon ladies arrived at the little church, the duchess found it was not so easy to carry out her intention, as the crowds outside were already dense.

"I believe there must be at least five thousand people here," the duchess whispered to Georgiana. Only minutes after their arrival the hearse appeared, harnessed to black horses decked with waving black ostrich plumes. Behind it came the duke's own carriage, empty, drawn by six bay horses, a footman leading his favorite hack, the pall-bearers on horseback, and a long line of carriages belonging to the nobility. Lit by torches and escorted by numbers of the Bedford tenantry, the procession had made its slow way from Woburn through the night.

Curious glances were cast at the two black-robed ladies, heavily veiled, attempting with hundreds of others to force their way into the church. The duchess pushed and shoved with the best of them, intent on gaining a seat in the front pew, and did not notice the disgraceful commotion about her. The escutcheons were torn from the hearse, the church windows had been shattered by the crowds, and the gangs of pickpockets were making a rich haul as the coffin, studded with thousands of silver nails and draped with a rich crimson velvet pall, was borne slowly down the aisle to the strains of the "Dead March" from *Saul*.

As the rector of Chenies began to intone the solemn words of the funeral service from the pulpit, covered in black and decorated with the late duke's coat of arms, the Duchess of Gordon ostentatiously brought her handkerchief to her eyes beneath her veil. When the rector went on to speak of the duke's virtues, she gave a loud sob.

"He was hospitable without prodigality, social without excess, exemplifying to the full the hereditary frankness of the house of Russell, an example to the aristocracy of what every nobleman should be . . ."

"Indeed, my love," the duchess murmured to Georgiana, "he was all that, poor Francis. Och, what a loss, my poor little widow."

Georgiana hastily directed her gaze at the upright leaden coffins in which lay the embalmed bodies of two Russells long since dead. Even her mother fell silent when the Duke of Bedford's coffin was lowered into the vault near that of Lady John Russell, whose funeral he had so recently attended.

At last the service came to an end, and the crowd surged out of the church, leaving Francis Russell, Duke of Bedford, Marquis of Tavistock, Earl of Bedford, Baron Russell of Chenies, Thornhaugh, and Howland of Streatham, alone with his deceased kin.

"Well, that's over," said the duchess complacently as she settled back into her carriage and tossed aside her black veil. "I have no doubt that tomorrow everyone will be talking about our attendance at the funeral. John Russell, I heard, was too overcome to be present."

"*I* am thinking of Francis," said Georgiana in a low voice. "Perhaps he is now better off than being married to me."

Instantly the duchess rounded on her daughter.

"How can you blether so? All *you* have to do is to show the world a becoming face of grief, while *my* work has to be done all over again—and not another unmarried duke in the whole country! I have every right to feel aggrieved."

For the remainder of their journey to London, the duchess sat in gloomy silence, interrupted only by brief exclamations of self-pity.

In the days that followed, Georgiana was hard put to obey her mother's bidding and wear the face of a mourning bride, but her public appearances were few, as the duchess considered it unseemly for her daughter to attend balls and routs. No such inhibitions affected the duchess herself, who everywhere continued to bewail the collapse of her plans, to the great amusement of the *ton*.

"Well, perhaps this will be a lesson to Jane Gordon and we'll hear a little less of her duchess-mania and her duchess daughters," was the general, unkind verdict. It was a mistaken one, however—it was never wise to underestimate the Duchess of Gordon's resources and resilience. So confirmed a gambler was sure to have a trump card up her sleeve, and she insinuated that she had one, although she admitted to herself that she was at a loss to find a new king of hearts.

Only a short while after the funeral, she was surprised to receive a letter from Woburn. When she had read it, she held it out to Georgiana.

"You will see, Georgy, that Lord John has written to ask my permission to call on you. He says he has something of great importance to impart to you."

"Thank you, Mama. I am reading the letter for myself."

"He asks if he may come tomorrow. How tiresome! Mr. Pitt is to speak on the peace negotiations in the House of Commons, and if I am not there to hear him he will be excessively put out."

She paused for a moment, then nodded decisively.

"In the circumstances, as Lord John is virtually still like a brother to you, I think it would be perfectly proper for you to receive him by yourself, but mind, Georgy," she warned, "that you show every mark of esteem and respect for the late duke."

"Yes, Mama," answered Georgiana dutifully in a flat voice, her thoughts busy with other things. The most absurd fancy had rushed unbidden to her mind—it *must* be absurd to so let her imagination run away with her. This was an idea she would do better to forget, she told herself sternly, although she was glad that her mother would not be present when Lord John paid his visit.

But when Georgiana sat alone in the vast drawing room at Buckingham House, watching the hands of the great gilded clock on the mantelpiece move with maddening slowness, she was now not so sure that she could receive Lord John comfortably without her mother's support. Anxious as she was to see him, she would be glad to have the interview over with, but it seemed hours before the door was flung open and Damour announced, "His Grace the Duke of Bedford."

Georgiana started, then recollected herself. Of course, Lord John, heir to all his brother's titles and vast estates, was now the Duke of Bedford. When he bowed over Georgiana's hand, he seemed as acutely embarrassed as she was herself, and he felt at a loss for what to say. After a few minutes' painful silence, at last he murmured, "It is a kind and delicate attention, ma'am, to wear mourning for my brother."

"It is no more than his due, sir—and *my mother* wishes it."

Georgiana hoped that the emphasis she put on her words would make John realize that her mourning was not by her own wish. The duchess had put her into a false position which she disliked excessively.

John began to pace up and down the room, clearly in great agitation of spirits, until he finally turned to face Georgiana and said, "You must be wondering, Lady Georgiana, why I have come to intrude on your grief. You must know that my brother has left me his personal property—we were on terms of the most affectionate and warmest intimacy."

John seemed to find some difficulty in continuing.

"Francis also left me a sealed letter which he instructed me to open after his death. I know you will understand that only recently have I been able to bring myself to do so—and that is why I am here now."

John's real grief made Georgiana feel ashamed. His mourning for his brother was so patently sincere, not like hers, which was worn as a mask to impress the world, but he was speaking and she gave him all her attention.

"I found a lock of my brother's hair enclosed in his letter, with the request that I should deliver it to you personally as a token of his regard. He charged me to express his profound regret that he would not live to wed you and his hope that you would think kindly of him. He wrote this letter and had the lock of his hair cut off only a few hours before his death, despite the great pain he was suffering—pain he endured so gallantly and uncomplainingly."

John's voice broke as he silently handed Georgiana the gold locket containing Francis's hair.

"I feel certain, Lady Georgiana, that in this last thought of you you will find proof of Francis's attachment. Even I was not aware of the depth of his feelings—of his affection for you. He did not easily speak of himself. This knowledge changes many things."

The tardy revelation of a devotion she had never suspected only increased Georgiana's shame and wretchedness. Holding the locket tightly in her hand, she faltered, "I am indeed greatly indebted to him, and to you, Lord John—or I should say 'Duke,' should I not?"

"Oh, no, Lady Georgiana." John's smile was sad. "Please call me by the old familiar name. I cannot yet accustom myself—I doubt if I shall ever be able to do so —to wearing my brother's title. It will be long before I can bear to hear myself addressed as the duke."

John paused, then said with peculiar emphasis, "I find it most bitter to borrow the titles and robes which always belonged to my brother." In a voice so low as to be almost inaudible, he added, "I find it hard, nay impossible, to take for myself anything that was his."

John avoided looking at Georgiana, but if his tone suggested some meaning he wished her to understand she failed to grasp it. She was still trying to puzzle out what it was when he took her hand in farewell.

"Although fate has deprived me of that happiness, Lady Georgy, I hope that in the future I may always regard you as the sister you would have been to me had Francis lived."

And, with no further word, he left the room.

Alone, turning the locket over and over again in her hand, Georgiana felt curiously desolate. So Francis had loved her after all! Had she known this, however, would it have lessened her reluctance to marry him? This question now demanded no answer, although it made her feel that she owed him the tribute of a decent, not a simulated, grief.

When the duchess returned from the House of Commons, she was so bubbling over with the news she brought with her that she failed to notice Georgiana's tear-stained face.

"What do you think, my love? Peace has been signed at Amiens! Peace with the French at last! Of course, it is all Mr. Pitt's doing, although he refuses to take the credit for it. What a marvelous man he is! Such a pity that he is disinclined to marry—"

"Oh, Mama, please! No more matches, I beg you. I had so much rather not be married at all than be surrounded by all this fuss and planning and what it leads to."

"What's all this about, Georgiana?" The duchess was displeased. "You are crying! Why? And what's that you're holding?"

"It's a lock of Francis's hair," sobbed Georgiana, unable any longer to restrain her tears. "Lord John—the duke—brought it to me. It was his brother's last wish that he should do so."

"Very proper, very pretty," approved the duchess as

she examined the locket. "I will find you a suitable chain, and you must wear it."

As Georgiana's tears flowed faster, the duchess was suddenly all motherly concern.

"There, there, my wee bairn, you're greeting for puir, dear Francis. And I know, however much you try to hide it, you are sad that you are not going to be a duchess. Now, dear Georgy, dinna' ye greet any longer, because your mama will contrive to see what can be done."

How useless to attempt to convince her mother that she was weeping with remorse, and for something unexplained, although what it was she did not know. All she knew was that she was thoroughly wretched. Let Mama think what she pleased! If it gratified her to believe her own fantasies, she might as well do so. Georgiana was tired of arguing with her.

Chapter Four

Rarely did Jane Gordon admit that she was mistaken, but now it seemed she had been. For some time she had been conscious that, by putting Georgiana into deep mourning, she was defeating her own ends. The duchess might boast of the scant attention she paid to what was said by the *ton*, but even she could not remain wholly insensitive to its criticism, and still more to its ridicule. She smarted under the mock solicitude of her great Whig rival, Georgiana, Duchess of Devonshire, who at a recent rout had said to her in a honey-sweet voice, "I trust, dear Jane, that you are feeling well? We looked in vain for you at the Theatre Royal last night. I had thought to see you there, since they were playing *Heigho for a Husband*."

All very well to ignore the Duchess of Devonshire's sneer, but it was all the more intolerable since Jane Gordon was desperate. Despite the brave face she wore, she was at a loss to find a husband sufficiently eligible for her daughter. Earls and viscounts were two a penny but

Georgiana, who had been betrothed to a duke, was not going to be permitted to make poor Madelina's mistake. Unthinkable that she should now be forced to descend so low in the peerage! Somehow a duke at least must be found for Georgy, but where?

Jane Gordon was thankful that attention was now riveted on the peace. This gave her a little respite and breathing space to concoct fresh plans.

"I think, dear Georgy, that the official proclamation of peace is such an occasion for national rejoicing that you may, in spite of your mourning, make a public appearance with propriety. Your sister Richmond has procured a window for us in St. James's Palace to watch the ceremony."

Delighted to be at liberty again after her enforced retirement, Georgiana tripped gaily beside her mother to St. James's, a few steps away from Buckingham House. Eagerly she leaned out of the window in Stable Yard to gaze at the solemn procession headed by the Sergeant Trumpeter with his mace and collar and the heralds and kings of arms in richly embroidered tabards and feathered hats.

"Do you not think that all this pageantry recalls the golden days of tilts and tournaments?" whispered Charlotte Richmond, only to be silenced by a frown from her mother as the trumpets sounded thrice and Garter King of Arms began his recital:

"By the king a proclamation! Whereas it has pleased Almighty God, in his great goodness, to put an end to the late bloody, extended, and expensive war ..."

And so on to the end. Then, preceded by the horse guards and beadles of Westminster carrying their staves of office, the heralds and kings of arms moved off on their gaily caparisoned horses to repeat the proclamation of peace at Temple Bar while the guns in Hyde Park and at the Tower of London roared their salutes.

"I did enjoy that, Mama," said Georgiana as they retraced their steps homeward.

"And I've no doubt that you will enjoy this evening even more. I hear the illuminations will be fabulous," replied her mother, pleased that, instead of her perpetual brooding, Georgiana was at last showing some interest in the world outside.

The duchess was right. Nothing like the evening's displays had ever been seen in London.

"Look, look, Mama," cried the Duchess of Manchester as the Gordon carriage with the Duchess of Gordon and four of her daughters inched its way through the dense crowds. Everyone was flocking to see the fireworks, which seemed to have set the sky on fire.

All the Gordon ladies turned in the direction in which Susan Manchester was pointing. Strung over the whole façade of the French ambassador's house in Portman Square was a brilliant transparency showing France and Britain uniting their hands. The thousands of candles made the piece a living, sparkling jewel festooned with light.

The Duchess of Gordon's carriage proceeded slowly through the West End, where the night sky showed an endless repetition of olive branches, stars, and catherine wheels. At Drury Lane Theatre, recently closed as a mark of respect to its late landlord, the Duke of Bedford, a model of a man-o'-war, flags and streamers floating from its topmasts, drew excited gasps from the good citizens of London and from the Duchess of Gordon's daughters.

Jane Gordon let their exclamations of wonder and delight and their chatter pass over her head. She had just been struck by an idea as brilliant as the fireworks themselves. She now gave them no more than an occasional glance as she revelled in her new plan. Depositing her daughters at their own homes on her way, she returned to Buckingham House, tired but excited by her new project, to be met by a broadly smiling Damour, who waved a newspaper under her nose.

"Your Grace, Your Grace, now I can return to France! I read in the *Gazette* that Bonaparte has amnestied the emigrants. At last I am free to return to my beloved country. Nobody knows, how sorely I have missed Paris these ten long years," he murmured, more to himself than to his mistress.

"But, Damour, you've been happy here? I understand that you are pleased that your country and mine are at last at peace, but why should you therefore want to leave us?"

As the full import of Damour's words sank in, Jane Gordon wailed, "What shall I do without you?"

"Alas, Your Grace, it is stronger than I am, my longing to see France again. Perhaps when I have done so I shall return to you, who knows?"

"But what shall we all do without you?" the duchess repeated helplessly.

"I am sure Your Grace will manage very well," answered Damour, a little impatiently.

"And when do you want to go?"

Damour bowed.

"Ah, I will await Your Grace's pleasure—if it is not too long delayed."

As she mounted the stairs to her room, all the duchess's previous elation vanished. Bedford's death had robbed her of a great triumph, and now Damour had announced his intention of leaving her. She had not the smallest expectation that, once he had returned to Paris, he would wish to come back to London.

Sleep eluded Jane Gordon as she tried to visualize what life would be without Damour to smooth her path. He had been far more a man of confidence than a mere servant.

Damour's skill in hairdressing, Damour's mastery of etiquette, Damour's knowledge of the Almanach de Gotha and of Europe—for he had disclosed that he had made the Grand Tour—had made him invaluable and herself the envy of the *ton*.

As she tossed and turned in bed, she recalled how magnificently Damour had coped when the Prince of Wales had descended on her house unannounced with a large party of friends to dance Scottish reels. How imperturbably Damour, challenged by Mr. Dundas, had led a Shetland pony into the drawing room and had not moved a muscle when the animal deposited on the floor indubitable proof of having made himself quite at home.

At last the duchess fell into a fitful sleep until, with morning and remembrance of her startling new plan, her spirits revived.

"I'm going to call on Mr. Pitt," she announced briskly.

Georgiana knew that, thanks be, the duchess would not insist on her daughter's company. She was heartily sick and tired of hearing about the peace, which was sure to be the subject of her mother's meeting with William Pitt. Georgiana did not quite know what she would like to hear, but certainly she was thoroughly discontented, especially since she saw no prospect of any improvement in her situation. What was the good of being pretty and having escaped from a distasteful marriage if the future was so blank?

As soon as she was dressed the duchess made her way to York Place in Baker Street, the new district springing up on the edge of Marylebone Fields, where William Pitt had taken up his residence after resigning the premiership after nearly twenty years in office.

This morning he was feeling far from well, and his early visitor was most unwelcome, even though she was his most ardent supporter. After the previous evening's celebration of his birthday, all he wanted was to be left alone to nurse his aching head. A thousand guests had with enormous enthusiasm drunk what seemed to have been a thousand toasts at Merchant Taylors' hall. Vaguely he recalled that, after the royal toasts, someone had proposed "The Wooden Walls of Old England" and "Lord Nelson and the Glorious Battle of the Nile," to the accompanying glees of "Britain's Best Bulwarks Are Her Wooden Walls" and "The Stormy Winds." Most flattering of all was the toast to himself, drunk with much waving of hats and a rousing three times three, "The Pilot Who Weathered the Storm."

William Pitt was quite moved by the knowledge that his dogged struggle against the French was so appreciatively recognized and that he had not worn himself to a shadow for an ungrateful country, but now he wished that this acclaim had not been accompanied by quite so much port. Even to think of the nautical toasts and glees made him feel seasick, while to be asked at this unreasonable hour to face the Duchess of Gordon, who would undoubtedly talk politics as loud and as fast as possible, made his head ache still more.

Impatiently the duchess waved away the footman's protests that his master, but lately out of bed, was still in his morning gown and nightcap.

"Och, I've seen many a gentleman in his nightcap before now! Announce to Mr. Pitt that it is the Duchess of Gordon who wishes to see him. Away with you, my man, and dinna' keep me waiting!"

When told who imperiously demanded to see him, William Pitt swore under his breath, then sighed wearily, "Show the duchess in."

Had his caller been anyone else, he would have insisted on being denied, but he could not risk offending Jane Gordon. He put up with her tiresome adulation and her loudly repeated conviction that he was one of the greatest men in the world because of her zeal in promoting his interests. No one but the Duchess of Gordon could use all the feminine arts to cajole or dragoon doubtful members of both Houses of Parliament to rally to the Tory cause. No one presided so well over his bachelor dinners as the duchess. No, he could not offend her, but when the duchess settled herself comfortably in her chair, his heart sank as he saw that she intended to make her visit a long one. In spite of his good resolutions, he winced at her forthright personality.

"Tell me, Mr. Pitt." The duchess leaned confidentially toward him as he sat slumped in an armchair. "Do you think this will be a lasting peace?"

"Ma'am, I am only an ex-prime minister, not a prophet," was the somewhat acid reply. "I earnestly hope, however, that it may prove to be so."

Ignoring Mr. Pitt's repressive tone, she continued her interrogation.

"And what do you think, really think, of General Bonaparte?"

William Pitt's aching head made it very difficult for him to concentrate, but it was evident that the duchess was in one of her most persistent moods and would be satisfied with nothing less than a considered answer.

"I think," he said slowly and cautiously, "that he is a young man greatly intoxicated with his own success."

Mr. Pitt allowed a wintry smile to appear on his face. After all, he himself had once been a very young man intoxicated with his own success.

"He may turn out to be a great and powerful influence for good. For that we must wait and see. He has certainly shown praiseworthy signs of good will by his peace with the Pope, by amnestying the emigrants, and by bringing the war to an end. More than that it is too early to say."

Jane Gordon waved aside the offer of a glass of Madeira, oblivious to the look of suffering William Pitt assumed. When pursuing her own train of thought, nothing was allowed to stand in its path.

"What do you think of this rumor that he may make himself emperor? Do you believe there is any truth in it? I had it from my daughter, Louisa Brome, who had it from her father-in-law, Lord Cornwallis. He says that in Paris it is the sole topic of conversation."

"It is possible," admitted Mr. Pitt grudgingly. "In any event, it cannot add to his power, which is already absolute."

To his surprise, the duchess seemed pleased by this answer.

"I must confess that I should very much like to see this great man."

"And why not, ma'am? So many of our compatriots are flocking to Paris that it will soon be an English colony."

"But do you think it safe?"

"If you mean by that, ma'am, will anyone cut off your head, I can assure you that it is most unlikely."

The duchess appeared content with this answer, but Mr. Pitt was not so himself. He wished savagely that someone would remove not Jane Gordon's head but her tongue, especially since she still gave no sign of an imminent departure.

"They say, do they not, that it is now unlikely that Madame Bonaparte will have any children, so, if the general does make himself emperor, who will succeed him?"

Mr. Pitt shrugged his shoulders so violently that he nearly lost his nightcap. He retrieved it with an irritated gesture. This was no time of day to be discussing Bonaparte's matrimonial affairs!

"I have no idea, ma'am. Bonaparte is a young man still and if he does not again expose himself to the hazards of war, he may well have many years before him. As for his successor, well, he has not yet made himself emperor, and for all I know, in spite of the rumors, he may never do so."

He hoped that he had succeeded at least in muzzling the duchess. So far as he himself was concerned, he did not care who made himself emperor of the French. Bonaparte might make himself Pope so long as William Pitt was allowed to lay his aching head on his pillow. He really must cut short this interview.

"My dear Duchess, I do not know what you have in your mind but, although I am always your servant to command, perhaps you will allow me to continue this discussion at some other time. I must confess that I am not feeling quite myself this morning."

Clapping his hand to his head as he did so, Mr. Pitt struggled out of his chair.

"Kindly give my respects to Lady Georgiana."

As she rose in her turn, the duchess's good humor was not a whit impaired.

"Ah, Mr. Pitt," she mourned as, to his infinite relief, she held out her hand in farewell, "when are we going to see you back at the helm?"

Mr. Pitt's smile was as chilly as the weather—not for many years had there been a May equal in severity to this one, with the temperature dropping nightly below the freezing point.

"Perhaps sooner than you think, Duchess. It depends, I believe, less on my colleagues in the House of Commons than on that young man over the water."

"All you tell me, dear Mr. Pitt," said the duchess as

she rustled out of the room, drawing her quilted pelisse about her, "confirms me in my view that General Bonaparte is a great man and that I must see him for myself."

Dear Mr. Pitt, thought the duchess indulgently as she drove back to Buckingham House well-satisfied with her interview. She was conscious of having neglected him of late, so busy had she been with Georgiana's affairs. As soon as her daughter's future was settled, the duchess determined, she would devote more attention to him, as he was obviously suffering from being out of office. What was the use of being called the most powerful woman in England if she did not succeed in again making him prime minister?

"Mama, you look frozen. Come and get warm," Georgiana greeted her mother from her own place by the fire, but the duchess waved her aside.

"Never mind that, Georgy. I'll soon get warm, and so will you when I tell you what I have decided. We are going to Paris!"

"To Paris, Mama? Why to Paris?"

"Because I say so, Georgy," answered the duchess automatically, and then continued in a rush, "From all I hear, Paris is now the place to be, quite the gayest city in Europe. Everyone is going—all our friends—and I should not wish to be behind the fashion. Mr. Pitt tells me it is quite safe; he does not think the peace will be broken. I have such a wish to see General Bonaparte."

Georgiana sighed. Obviously Mama had found a new hero, and she looked forward gloomily to having the general's name dinned at her without pause. Her spirits rose, however, when the duchess added, "You cannot go out much here because you are in mourning, but in Paris it cannot signify—the French are only foreigners! Oh, we will enjoy ourselves, I promise you. Even Mr. Pitt is convinced that General Bonaparte is a great man!"

Georgiana made no immediate reply as she gazed into the leaping flames of the fire, turning the duchess's plan over in her mind. To her surprise, she decided that she did not dislike it. A change of scene might lift this unaccountable depression which she could not shake off. Nothing seemed to restore her normal good spirits, although she could not think why.

As Georgiana looked up at her mother's radiant face, which beamed with pleasure, she felt a little guilty. After all, it was Mama who had been so bitterly disappointed by Francis's death; Georgiana did not have the heart to throw cold water on her scheme when she was clearly so eager to go to Paris and so pleased with herself for thinking of this journey. But Georgiana had another, more personal reason, for approving a stay in Paris. Surely there Mama would not be able to indulge her passion for matchmaking, because she would not want her daughter to marry a Frenchman and live so far away from her.

With a smile, Georgiana raised her head.

"Very well, Mama, we will go to Paris, and we'll show the French just how gay the gay Gordons can be!"

"That's my Georgy, that's my bairn," exclaimed the duchess, and folded her daughter in an embrace. "Now, to work! Ring the bell for Damour and we will arrange our journey. We shall leave as soon as possible."

But, to the duchess's annoyance, an early departure was not to be. Not only the British but also the Russians were flocking in such numbers to Paris that it proved exceedingly difficult to find a suitable mansion for their stay. The duchess, of course, intended to keep magnificent state.

Ten times a day she harried Damour.

"You are quite sure, Damour, that no letter has come from the agent in Paris?"

"You're quite sure that the Mouton d'Or is the best inn in the town?" the duchess asked Damour anxiously.

"The Grande Place is the heart of Spa, Your Grace, and the Mouton d'Or is always patronized by the Duchess of Devonshire on her frequent visits."

"I hope to God Georgiana Devonshire isn't coming to Spa this year!" exclaimed the duchess in alarm. "I have quite enough of her and her Charles James Fox at home."

"Your Grace need have no fears," Damour soothed her. "I made it my business to ascertain Her Grace of Devonshire's plans for the summer; she is remaining at Chatsworth."

"Damour, I don't know how you manage to think of everything. You must never leave me, never!"

The Gordon ladies quickly settled into the routine of a watering place. After the morning's outing to swallow the sulfur waters, which tasted of rotten eggs, the duchess and her daughter strolled in the charming Parc des Sept Heures. Here they were sure to meet all their friends, as the town was full to bursting with both English and French. In the evenings, while Georgiana, suitably chaperoned, attended concerts and plays at the theater, the duchess indulged her passion for hazard at the Salon Levoz, but without losing sight of her main objective.

No one at Spa was remotely eligible for Georgiana, so she sought out her French acquaintances to bombard them with questions.

"Do you really think Napoleon Bonaparte will make himself emperor?"

A shrug was generally the sole answer.

"But," the duchess persisted, "he has been created consul for life, has he not?"

"*Mais oui*, Madame la Duchesse, it is true that it could well be the first step to a throne."

Immediately the duchess was off on another tack.

"But since he has no children, who will succeed him? It is a fact, is it not, that Madame Bonaparte will have no more children?"

"He has brothers, Madame, but they are not worth much. And he has adopted the son of Madame Bonaparte, Eugène de Beauharnais."

"So that it is very possible that he might choose Monsieur de Beauharnais to succeed him?"

"You go too fast, Madame la Duchesse! As yet the general is only First Consul. We must wait and see."

The duchess might counsel others to wait and see but her natural impatience demanded immediate action, and she disliked having her own words turned against her.

A month at Spa was sufficient for the duchess, who had exhausted all its delights. After a critical inspection of Georgiana's looks, she pronounced herself satisfied.

"I was quite right to bring you here, because undoubtedly the waters have done you good—you look like my own wee Georgy again."

Then, as an afterthought, she remarked, "You are not wearing your locket. Where is it?"

Georgiana was immediately on the defensive.

"You said, Mama, that there comes a time when one may no longer give way to grief."

"Did I indeed say so, Georgy?"

"Yes, Mama, you did—and so I left the locket at home."

For once the duchess made no further comment. After all, she reasoned, Francis was dead, and nothing now could bring him back to life. On the whole, it was probably better to turn Georgiana's mind to the future rather than let her dwell on the past.

"You *are* looking forward to going to Paris, aren't you, Georgy?"

"I am indeed, Mama. I'm tired of Spa, the waters are

obnoxious, and everyone here is so elderly. All they talk about is their ailments. I want to meet people of my own age and go to balls and dance. I want to enjoy myself!"

"And so you shall! I have no doubt that the Duchess of Gordon and her daughter will be made very welcome in Paris."

Chapter Five

Naturally the Duchess of Gordon and Lady Georgiana took their place in the front rank of the many thousands of foreign visitors who had taken Paris by storm. No one boasted such rich liveries, such gorgeously emblazoned armorial bearings on carriages so luxurious, and no one entertained so magnificently as Jane Gordon.

The duchess was not one who lived in cheap lodgings, grumbled about the high prices, and haggled about the cost of everything, finding fault with the cold, the heat, and the bad beds. Which is not to say she found everything to her taste, but with heroic restraint she curbed her unruly tongue, determined to say or do nothing to wound French sensibilities, a resolution easier to make than to keep.

"You like the house, Your Grace?" asked Damour as he showed her around the Hôtel de Richelieu.

"Delightful, Damour, quite delightful. You could not

have found me anything better—and that little square is
so pretty. The Place des Vosages, you call it?"

"No, no, Your Grace, not *Vosages*—Vosges—Place
des Vosges."

Damour was not alone in his hopeless struggle with the
duchess's French pronunciation.

"The Duchess of Gordon talks nonsense in the worst
French and the most illiterate Scotch I ever heard," complained Colonel Thomas Everest to his traveling companion, Hilary Grant.

"Come, come, Thomas, it's surely not as bad as all that."

" 'Pon my word, it is. You can afford to be complacent
about it because you are not at her beck and call, as I
am."

The duchess had made Colonel Everest's acquaintance
at Spa and, perceiving him to be a gentleman and, like
herself, bound for Paris, had commandeered him as an
escort until she could find someone better.

By the time the early spring of 1803 had clothed Paris
in a mist of green leaves, the duchess and Georgiana considered themselves as old inhabitants and an accepted part
of Paris society. Happily, the duchess was unaware that
her eccentricities and her less-than-ducal manners made
her a rich source of amusement, but in Georgiana no one
could find a fault; her beauty and grace were univer-
sally admired.

"I am so thankful," the duchess told Damour, "that
Lady Georgy has shaken off her low spirits. She has made
a great impression on all the nicest young men in Paris,
which, of course, was no more than I expected."

No girl could for long remain untouched by the delicate compliments and heady attentions showered on her.
Georgiana had blossomed into greater assurance through
this admiration while the duchess basked in her success.
Only two things marred Jane Gordon's contentment. First,

she was chagrined to find that she was not the only British duchess in Paris, and then was doubly annoyed when Lady Yarmouth arrived to challenge her preeminence as a hostess.

"Is it not absurd," Jane Gordon complained to all and sundry, "that the British ambassadress clings to the title of duchess although since she married Lord Whitworth *en deuxièmes noces* she is not really entitled to parade as the widowed Duchess of Dorset! You may be sure that, whenever I meet her, I make a point of addressing her as Lady Whitworth."

The duchess was not in the least disturbed that, by insisting on this point, she became a most unpopular visitor to the British embassy. Others might need the ambassador's patronage, but not she!

The duchess confided her grievances about Lady Yarmouth to Colonel Everest.

"Who does Maria Yarmouth think she is? That's just it—who is she? Maria Fagniani, the daughter of a ballet dancer or some such, and doesn't know whether her father is George Selwyn or the Duke of Queensberry. And she sets herself up to be a queen of Paris society —well, she'll find she's met her match in Jane Gordon, mark my words."

"If only the duchess did not blurt out everything which comes into her head," moaned the colonel to Mr. Grant. "And she is so energetic that I have the utmost difficulty in keeping up with her!"

"Oh, come now, Thomas. You know that the duchess takes you into circles to which you yourself would have no *entrée*."

Hilary Grant failed to add that, however tired his friend professed himself to be of Jane Gordon's exuberance and incessant calls on him, he was far too great a snob not to be gratified by her confidences. Indiscreet though she so often was, in general the duchess knew how to keep silent about her real objective in Paris and the steps she was taking toward achieving it.

"Georgy," she said with studied carelessness after they had been in Paris a short time. "Mourning becomes you greatly, you look bewitching in black, but perhaps it is time to lighten it. Yes, I think it will now be enough for you to wear just a knot of black ribbons on your gown —General Bonaparte likes ladies to wear white. I am told that Madame Bonaparte always does so."

Great though her admiration for the general was, in reality the duchess cared less for his preferences than for her sudden realization that any prospective husband seeing the girl of his choice wearing deep mourning for another man would hardly be encouraged.

Having thus finally dismissed the Duke of Bedford from her mind, the duchess was ready to exert herself in more profitable directions. She paid a morning call on Madame Junot, wife of the governor of Paris and a leading figure in French society.

"Georgy, dear Madame Junot has given me tickets to witness General Bonaparte's review this week. As you know I am longing to see him," she announced on her return.

This was now the duchess's favorite remark, and she repeated it so often that already Georgiana was heartily tired of it.

General Bonaparte's weekly reviews at the Tuileries were a great attraction for the foreigners in Paris. Even those who spoke most disparagingly of "the Corsican" were thrilled as he rode on his white charger down the motionless ranks drawn up on the great Place du Carrousel. Dressed in the blue coat faced with white of his consular guard and the black beaver hat with its small tricolor cockade, which he wore like a crown, the general saluted the colors. As the regiments marched past in open order, the drums beat and fifes blared. The English spectators, forgetting that General Bonapartè had so lately been their enemy, joined enthusiastically in the crowd's applause as artillery and cavalry galloped off the parade ground and the general rode back into the Tuileries at the end of the parade.

"Did you see dear General Junot at the First Consul's side?" the duchess asked Georgiana with a touch of self-consciousness. "What a handsome man he is to be sure —and so obliging."

Georgiana suppressed a smile. General Junot's attentions to her mother amused her, but the duchess's *tendre* for him did not. Surely Mama was not indulging in a *flirt* at her age? But that was precisely what the duchess was doing, justifying it by telling herself that, as one of the most influential men in Paris, General Junot was a valuable connection. In reality, she was flattered by his open admiration of her mature charms.

Urged on by her husband, Madame Junot was at pains to show the Gordons every courtesy, and a charming note accompanied the cards she procured for them so that they could attend one of Madame Bonaparte's receptions. Although the invitation was no more than was due to her rank, the duchess was cock-a-hoop.

"I'm so longing to see General Bonaparte at close quarters! What a great man he is—how I should like to see him breakfast in Ireland, dine in London, and sup at Gordon Castle."

Georgiana, thankful that no one but herself heard this foolish remark, turned her mother's thoughts in another direction by asking, "What am I to wear, Mama, to go to the Tuileries?"

"White, of course, and perhaps,"—the duchess hesitated —"no black ribbons. You must be in your best looks."

And as she made her curtsey to Madame Bonaparte, Georgiana did indeed look radiant.

"Madame la Duchesse, I am delighted to welcome you and your charming daughter."

Josephine Bonaparte, installed in almost royal state in the magnificent salons of the Tuileries, greeted the Gordon ladies with the amiability and graciousness she was noted for. Then she called forward her daughter, Hortense, who was married to the general's youngest brother, Louis Bonaparte.

"Hortense, I present to you Lady Georgiana Gordon. You may practice your English with her, and Lady Georgiana will speak French to you."

The two girls looked shyly at each other; then, as each began to speak hesitantly in the other's language, they burst out laughing. Soon, the duchess noted with approval, they were chattering away together like old friends.

Excellent! she thought. Most useful to have young Madame Louis on one's side.

General Bonaparte's welcome to the duchess was neither gracious nor cordial. He treated her with that particular brand of rudeness which was all his own.

"I dislike women who meddle in politics," he said pointedly with a baleful glare.

This was certainly true, but Napoleon had another reason for his hostility. He greatly admired Charles James Fox, who had lately visited Paris. Since the general was very well informed by his spies, he was well aware how ardent a champion the Duchess of Gordon was of Fox's rival, William Pitt.

"Far better mind your distaff or your needle," the general adjured her repressively, but this brusqueness failed to offend her.

"Strength and energy are what I admire in a man," she

remarked that evening to Colonel Everest. "You have only to look about you to see what the First Consul has done for France. Order has replaced the disorder of the revolution, and a high moral tone the license it encouraged."

Colonel Everest tittered. To hear the duchess, no moralist herself, praising a high moral tone was richly amusing. He must remember to tell Hilary.

"I hear that in one thing only has he failed and that is in purging the Palais Royal. Is it really such a sink of iniquity?"

"The very fount of evil," was the colonel's solemn reply.

"Nevertheless, I should very much like to see it. Will you escort me there?"

"Positively no! It distresses me to refuse you, Duchess, but you could not possibly be seen there."

"Silly old woman," muttered Jane Gordon, and she determined to visit the Palais Royal alone if necessary, although at the moment she was too busy. General Junot had taken to haunting the Hôtel de Richelieu, and luckily Georgiana was spending so much time with Hortense Bonaparte that the duchess was free to enjoy his attentions without her daughter's disapproving presence. Occasionally she felt slightly guilty that she was neglecting her.

"You *are* enjoying yourself, aren't you, Georgy?" she would then ask anxiously, always to receive the same reply.

"Oh, Mama, it is heaven here! I did not believe it possible to enjoy myself so much!"

But, although the duchess kept this to herself, she intended that Georgiana should enjoy herself still more. Because of this, she assumed an indifference she was far from feeling when one day Georgiana remarked, "Hortense says that she would like me to meet her brother, who has just returned from a mission to Italy."

On their very next visit to the Tuileries, where now they were frequent guests, Josephine Bonaparte called forward a handsome young man, turning as she did so to the duchess.

"Permit me, Madame la Duchesse, to introduce to you my son, Eugène. I hope that he will be allowed to stay with us for some time in Paris, and that duty will not call him away again."

As the young Vicomte de Beauharnais stooped to kiss Jane Gordon's hand, she drew in her breath sharply as she eyed him up and down, assessing his points as if he were a horse whose purchase she was considering. He was tall, good-looking, with a sweet expression and steadfast eyes, decidedly aristocratic in bearing—altogether an admirable young man!

What made him even more admirable in the duchess's eyes was his obvious appreciation of Georgiana's beauty, and that he immediately engaged her in conversation. She clearly found it pleasing, since her silvery laugh was constantly ringing out. Soon the duchess was saying airily to Colonel Everest, "You know, young Eugène de Beauharnais is an excellent young man, a devoted son, and, I hear, very popular with the army."

"And very attentive to Lady Georgiana," was the colonel's answer, given not without a touch of malice, which the duchess failed to remark.

"Yes, indeed! He is one of the most persistent of her cavaliers. Whenever we join in the evening promenade in the Bois de Boulogne, we are sure of meeting Monsieur de Beauharnais. As soon as he sees our carriage—I am sure he must lie in wait for it"—the duchess gave a self-conscious laugh—"he rides up to us immediately. He looks so dashing in his uniform."

"I myself think it a very showy dress, ma'am. I belong to the artillery," was the colonel's stiff rejoinder. He was always glad of any opportunity to contradict the duchess when he might do so without offending her.

"Well, I don't suppose you can help it now," she answered impatiently, anxious only to talk about her own interests. "I suppose it is now too late for you to exchange into another arm."

"I have no wish to do so, ma'am."

"Oh, well, *chacun à son goût*, as they say here."

Thomas Everest winced at the duchess's French pronunciation, and soon after took his leave, but he would have been chagrined to know that she scarcely noticed his departure. In her mind's eye she saw Eugène, forcing his horse to a walking pace, his hand resting lightly on the carriage door, making Georgiana trill with laughter at his droll stories and the latest Paris gossip. Georgy, of course, had very quickly become proficient in French. But what pleased the duchess even more were the increasingly insistent rumors that General Bonaparte would very shortly proclaim himself emperor of the French. She had seen for herself how Madame Bonaparte used every art to conceal her age.

"If that woman is still capable of bearing children, then so am I," the duchess said to herself. "As for the general, they say he's incapable of fathering a child. Why, he's not known to have even a by-blow. His brothers are nothing but a parcel of nincompoops hanging on to his coattails, but Eugène's a very different kettle of fish. He possesses all his mother's charm, and that indefinable something which is the hallmark of an aristocrat. If I were the general, *I* would not look further for a worthy successor."

The duchess's excitement kept pace with Eugène's increasingly marked intentions. Now Colonel Everest's complaints to his friend were a daily occurrence.

"Really, Hilary, the duchess is becoming so unbearable that I shall have to give up her society. She should be called the Duchess of Gorgon, not Gordon."

"I don't suppose you mean that," answered Mr. Grant drily. "How can you be so taken in? Can't you see that she thinks she's succeeding in making a match of it between that girl of hers and young de Beauharnais? My own opinion is that, if it comes to the crunch, she'll find the general a harder nut to crack than she imagines."

"You may be right," said Colonel Everest doubtfully, and then brightened. "What's the betting?"

Hilary Grant shook his head.

"I wouldn't bet on it. By the way, how much did you drop at the Salon des Etrangers last night?"

"A few hundred francs, damn it, but at any rate the Gorgon has stopped insisting that I take her to the Palais Royal. Good God! that would be a scandal indeed!"

Colonel Everest was mistaken, however. The duchess had by no means forgotten her wish to visit the Temple of Sin, only at the moment all her efforts were concentrated on achieving her ambition. Personal indulgence must go by the board, except, of course, for General Junot! The duchess fondly pictured Georgiana as the Vicomtesse de Beauharnais, with the dazzling prospect of one day being the Empress Georgiana before her. And why should she not be royal? Wasn't Charlotte's husband, the Duke of Richmond, a descendant of Charles II of England and his French mistress, Louise de Kerouailles? Jane Gordon flattered herself that her grandchildren had royal blood, even if it had flowed first through the veins of a bastard.

"Georgy," announced the duchess imperatively on their return from a ball. "You must have some dancing lessons."

"Why, Mama?" yawned Georgiana, wriggling her tired feet in her sandals. "I thought I danced pretty well."

"And so you do, my love, Scottish reels and English country dances, but the steps of these quadrilles they dance here are very complicated—more like those in ballets. I'll arrange for you to have lessons with Monsieur Vestris—they call him the king of the dance, you know."

The duchess's decision that Georgiana should study with Vestris had nothing to do with improving her knowledge of the dance. Since she was convinced that the fast-ripening love affair between Georgiana and Eugène needed but a push to bring it to fruition, her mother was anxious that the young people should spend as much time as possible in each other's company. Who knew how long Eugène would remain in Paris? In pursuit of her plan, the duchess decided to pay another morning call on Madame Junot.

"Dear Madame Junot," she gushed, exerting all her charm. "I have heard so much about the beauty of General Bonaparte's sisters, but as yet I have not met any of them. Madame Leclerc is, of course, on her way back from San Domingo—so sad that the general died and left her a young widow. It happened to my Georgiana, too—you know she was intended for the Duke of Bedford."

The duchess heaved a long sigh as Laure Junot, hiding a smile, nodded sympathetically. No one in Paris had been allowed to remain unaware of Georgiana's betrothal to the duke—her sad story had been trumpeted everywhere by her mother. What did the duchess want now, wondered Laure, arching her long, swanlike neck. She had certainly not come merely to repeat a long-familiar story.

"Now that the general's family is out of mourning for General Leclerc, I suppose they will resume their usual entertainments," said the duchess carelessly. "Madame

Murat, I hear, has just arrived from Italy. I should like to meet her."

Madame Junot felt she owed the duchess some return for the vast amusement she gave to Paris society—and it would please Junot if she did the duchess a favor. His attentions to Jane Gordon were, of course, ridiculous, but if her overblown charms appealed to him, this little *affaire* was less alarming than certain others. Whatever object the duchess was pursuing—and by now everyone in Paris had a pretty good idea of what it was—if Laure did not help her someone else would.

"I shall be charmed to introduce you to Madame Murat, Madame la Duchesse—we are great friends. I have known her ever since she first came to Paris. She is a lovely creature, like a half-opened rose, and I am sure she will be delighted with your daughter. They are the same age—we are all the same age, of course, but in France we marry very young."

This sly dig at the matchmaking duchess whose daughter, although nearly twenty-one was still unmarried, went unnoticed. Caroline Murat's age and beauty were of no interest to her. All she cared about was that the First Consul's sister gave splendid entertainments at her palatial home in Paris, the Hôtel de Thélusson, and that the prettiest young women and handsomest young men in the city competed for the honor of dancing in her quadrilles. The many rehearsals required to bring the dancers to perfection offered excellent opportunities for them to meet with little or no chaperonage.

Fortified with Laure Junot's introduction, Jane Gordon called on Madame Murat.

"Dear Madame Murat," she cooed, "I am very happy to meet you at last. I am such a great admirer of your brother. I would like to offer you a length of my Gordon tartan silk, which I hope you will do me the honor of accepting. It is the genuine article, not," she added tactlessly, "an imitation, although I must say it is gratifying that French ladies are so enamored of my *écossais* that I have set the fashion in Paris as well as in London."

Caroline Murat evidenced no sign of her amusement as, with a graciousness that imitated her sister-in-law, Josephine's, she accepted Jane Gordon's gift. She was not in the least surprised when the real object of the visit was revealed.

"I hope," said the duchess, "that you will allow me to present to you my daughter Georgiana. Vestris, you know, considers her to be one of his very best pupils."

For a moment Madame Murat hesitated, then shrugged the pretty shoulders of which she was so proud.

"It would give me—and I am sure my guests also— Madame la Duchesse, much pleasure if your daughter would consent to take part in the quadrille I am arranging for my next ball."

"Och, ye'll no' regret it, ma'am," exclaimed the duchess, breaking into broad Scots, as she always did when excited. "She's a bonny dancer is my Georgy."

Although Madame Murat did not understand the duchess's Scots her satisfaction was obvious. Damour, of course, immediately seized on the significance of the invitation when the duchess, in high glee, informed him of it, adding, "I have no doubt that Lady Georgy will beat them all at their own game."

"Especially since I hear that Monsieur de Beauharnais is also to dance in the quadrille." Damour almost winked.

"Oh, you must not say so, Damour," answered the duchess. Once again, however, she silently thanked heaven that he had not, as she had feared he might, disappeared on their arrival in Paris. Damour had his own ways of finding out things, and his private intelligence service was of the utmost use to her.

Ever since the Gordons had been caught up in the social

whirl, the duchess had had little opportunity to question Damour about his feelings at being back in Paris, but now she asked curiously, "Are you happy to be home again, Damour?"

A slight shadow crossed his face as he said slowly, "Very happy, Your Grace, although things here are not now what they once were. This *hôtel*, for instance..." He stopped abruptly. "Is there anything further Your Grace wishes? It is urgent that I now speak with the chef."

So Damour still refused to reveal anything about his past! Well, the duchess had other things on her mind, so she had to be content that, under his iron rod, her household in Paris ran even more smoothly than in London. All that really mattered was that Georgy bubbled over with gaiety. She was so different from the sad, withdrawn girl the duchess had brought from London.

"Oh Mama," Georgiana exclaimed after a rehearsal of the quadrille. "We are having the greatest fun! I am not allowed to tell you what the quadrille is to be, because it is a secret, but you will see how amusing it is when the time comes."

The duchess regarded it as a most favorable sign that Georgiana rarely mentioned Eugène, but her daughter's confidences were unnecessary, since Damour faithfully reported to her. He informed her that it was always Monsieur de Beauharnais who handed Georgiana into the carriage and lingered as long as possible before reluctantly bidding her good-bye.

At last, after fifteen rehearsals, Monsieur Vestris expressed himself as satisfied with the dancers and a date was fixed for the performance of the quadrille.

"Think, Mama! The First Consul and Madame Bonaparte are to be present. Am I not lucky to be taking part?"

"Pooh! It is not every day that a Lady Georgiana Gordon honors a Madame Murat, but I am delighted that her dear brother will be there. I have a great deal I wish to say to him."

So great was the press of people at the ball that the duchess was unable to get near General Bonaparte. She therefore contented herself with admiring Georgiana's graceful dancing in the complicated figures of the quadrille, the theme of which was a living game of chess.

Great squares of blue and red had been laid out on the ballroom floor. The pawns, pretty young women in short skirts with little aprons, were attended by red or blue knights, while the fattest men in Paris society had been cajoled into playing the castles, disguised in stiff cardboard tabards. To Georgiana had fallen the signal honor of dancing the Red Queen to Eugène's Red King, both of them sparkling with rubies borrowed from all the jewel cases in Paris.

As the duchess proudly watched Georgiana's movements, directed by two masked magicians waving their wands, she could not resist whispering to Colonel Everest, for whom she had procured an invitation, "How wise of Madame Murat to choose Georgy as the Red Queen. I am sure no one else could dance those intricate steps as well as she does."

For once the duchess's fondness had not led her to exaggerate. Georgiana's skill and grace were admired by all but one of the guests.

"That young woman to whom Eugène is paying a lot of attention," murmured General Bonaparte with a frown to Laure Junot. "It is the daughter of that stupid woman, the Duchess of Gordon, no?"

"Yes, General. Do you not think her pretty?"

Napoleon Bonaparte snorted.

"She will end like her mother, fat and blowsy. They say *she* was once a beauty. Pah! Do not annoy me, Madame Junot, by bringing that young woman and my son together. I hear that they frequently meet at your house."

Laure Junot tossed her head saucily.

"I shall receive whom I wish, General."

Since she had known Napoleon Bonaparte from the time of his first appearance in Paris as a threadbare young lieutenant, Laure Junot was one of the few who neither trembled in his presence nor submitted slavishly to his wishes.

"Little pest," muttered the general, although a smile lurked in his eyes. "You will listen to what I say. Eugène may have as many opera dancers as he chooses, but the young ladies of the *monde* he will leave alone! It is not my wish that he should be inveigled into marriage. He is too young, and I have other plans for him."

But even General Bonaparte's keen eyes failed to perceive how deeply Eugène had fallen in love, and that it was now too late to nip this love affair in the bud. He did not know that Georgiana had never seemed so happy as when she was in Eugène's company. Although the duchess marked this fact with great satisfaction, she forbore to ply her daughter with questions. She chose to think that Georgiana must be as elated as herself at the prospect of a matrimonial prize as great as—no, greater than —Francis, Duke of Bedford.

Terrific applause greeted the end of the quadrille, and even the First Consul signified his approbation.

"I congratulate you, Caroline," he told his sister. "The quadrille was very well devised. You may give another some time soon and I will come to see it."

Caroline Murat was gratified that her brother appeared to realize how useful a social asset she was to him. Her secret hope was always that he would look no further for a successor than his brother-in-law, the brilliant cavalry general, and of course, his wife, Caroline.

How crowns become them both, thought the duchess as

Eugène led Georgiana to the buffet to hand her a glass of wine. He bent his dark head to her fair one with its diadem of winking rubies.

"What would you say, Lady Georgiana, if I gave a ball in my new house?"

"I would say it sounds delightful, Monsieur de Beauharnais. But where is your house? Do you not live with your mother at the Tuileries?"

Eugène shook his head.

"No. I have set up my own establishment in the *hôtel* my stepfather so kindly bought for me. It is in the Rue de Lille in the Faubourg-St. Germain. If you promise to come, I shall give a splendid ball and perhaps you will honor me with the first two dances and the supper dance and the last two dances and . . ."

Georgiana held up a protesting hand.

"Stop, stop, Monsieur de Beauharnais! It sounds as if you want me to dance with you the whole evening."

"But I do, milady." Eugène smiled tenderly. "Our steps match so perfectly and you are so exquisite a dancer —and not only a dancer—I should like to dance with you forever."

Georgiana blushed rosily.

"No one but you says such pretty things to me, Monsieur de Beauharnais."

"Do they not? Tell me who they are and I will call them out!"

Eugène was half in jest, half in earnest, and Georgiana looked alarmed, but she was reassured by Eugène's smile as again he bent toward her to say softly, "Must you always call me by that cold and formal 'Monsieur de Beauharnais'? Will you not call me Eugène—or is it that I ask too much?" he added anxiously in his quaint English.

As if debating a very weighty matter, Georgiana eyed him solemnly while Eugène assumed a worried expression. It soon cleared when, with a roguish smile, she answered, "Very well. I will call you Eugène if you will call me Georgy. That is what my friends call me. Georgiana is such a long name."

"I think Georgiana is a very beautiful name, but if you prefer I will call you George-y. There is a famous actress in Paris called George—she is a great favorite with my stepfather."

"You do not speak of the general as your father, only your stepfather. Why?"

"Because to me he is first of all the general. I am devoted to him, but I would not presume to call him *mon père*. He has, however, been a real father to me and to Hortense since he adopted us when he married our mother."

"Madame Bonaparte is so charming," ventured Georgiana shyly, to be rewarded by a most grateful look from Eugène.

"I am so happy that you like her, George-y," he pronounced proudly. "And she likes you. She told me so. It will make everything so much . . ."

He stopped abruptly, and Georgiana, a little troubled, did not ask him to finish what he had been saying. She liked Eugène very much, but as yet she was not certain if she wanted to like him more. In the meantime, she was happy to enjoy his society and his attentions, while the duchess heroically did not ask whether Eugène had yet declared himself.

"Tonight we are dining with Monsieur Cambacérès, Georgy," she said one evening, hoping that Georgiana would say that Eugène had made other plans for her, but no.

"Oh, Mama, I do not know how I shall keep my countenance! Fancy having a hollow cut out of your dining table to fit your paunch!"

Briefly the duchess echoed Georgiana's peals of

laughter, but quickly recovered from her mirth to reprove her daughter.

"Paunch or no paunch, Monsieur Cambacérès keeps the best table in Europe, and you are not to laugh at him, Georgy. He is a very important political personage. And the truffled turkey we had there the other evening," she added dreamily, "was better than any I ever tasted."

"I am not at all as interested in food as you are, Mama."

"Nor was I, my Georgy, at your age. I thought only of feeding on love. Is that what you are doing?"

In spite of all her good resolutions, Jane Gordon could not resist asking, but Georgiana made no answer, and rashly the duchess went on.

"There is someone who is thinking a great deal about love—love for Georgiana Gordon—and I am sure I have no need to tell you whom I mean."

She waved aside Georgiana's attempt to interrupt.

"He's made for you, Georgy! He'll make you a marvelous husband, and think what a position you'll have when the general makes himself emperor."

"Nonsense, Mama. You know I care nothing for position. I want only to be happy."

"Eugène would make any woman happy . . ."

"He is indeed wholly charming, but . . ."

The duchess bit back her rejoinder. Her unruly tongue had again run away with her. She consoled herself, however, that at least Georgiana had not flown out at her, as she so often did when marriage was in question.

At the next reception at the Tuileries, Jane Gordon noticed with satisfaction that Eugène at once went to Georgiana's side and then turned to see his mother's reaction.

"I've an ally there at least," she said to herself, observing Josephine smile at the handsome young couple and at her son's glowing face.

"I don't anticipate any trouble with Madame Bonaparte," the duchess later told Colonel Everest, whom she had now made a party to her hopes. "Josephine is an aristocrat who knows birth and breeding when she sees it. Before the revolution she would have been overjoyed to get the daughter of a British duke for her son, and now the French have cut off the heads of nearly all their own dukes, I should think she'd be even more delighted."

"The odds seem to be shortening," reported Thomas Everest to his friend. "It really does look as if the duchess will pull it off."

"Well, Thomas," was the languid reply, "it may be so, but it cannot be of any great moment to us. It isn't as if either of us comes within the duchess's orbit. With no more daughters to marry off, I'm sure she'll be wholly at a loss."

"Don't you believe it, Hilary. I've never met a woman with so much energy. I wish to God she hadn't got her claws into me. I can tell you, I'm quite worn out with squiring her to balls and routs. She never seems to want to go to bed."

"Perhaps not with you, Thomas," Hilary Grant sniggered, "but what about General Junot?"

"Don't you know? He's transferred his affections to Lady Yarmouth, and the duchess is mad as fire. It's all very wearing. When she's not ramming young de Beauharnais down my throat as an eligible husband for Lady Georgiana, who, I must say, is a nice, unspoiled girl, she's railing at Maria Yarmouth until I am exhausted."

"Nevertheless, Thomas," said Hilary slyly, "the connection is not one you would wish to give up. The Duchess of Gordon is a power in the land."

Colonel Everest looked somewhat annoyed and murmured something under his breath. His friend then remarked, "I suppose you've received a card for Lady Yarmouth's ball?"

"Naturally," was the stiff reply.

Later in the day, the Duchess of Gordon asked Colonel Everest the same question.

"I see," he said to her, with a bit of malice, "that she has hired Frascati's—there could not be a greater coup."

"Do you not think so, Colonel?" Jane Gordon replied, "Wait and see. Of course, Maria sent me a card—she could scarcely avoid doing so—but I have half a mind not to go. I suppose I *shall* go, since if I did not it would look as if that insufferable woman had not invited us."

"But *her* daughters are not yet of marriageable age," the Colonel blurted out, to be rewarded by a glare from the duchess, who remained out of charity with him until Lady Yarmouth's ball restored her good humor.

"What an insipid affair that turned out to be," she said with a pleased smile to Georgiana, on their return that evening. "I suppose Maria thought to keep it select by asking so few people, and no doubt she is acquainted only with the English here. And how late the supper was served! If I hadna' been starving, I should have left long since. Anyway, I won a large sum at hazard from General Berthier, dear General Bonaparte's chief of staff. He may be a brilliant staff officer, but I hope he marshals his troops with more skill than he does his dice!"

The duchess chuckled at her joke, but Georgiana yawned; she had very little interest in games of chance.

"I noticed that Monsieur de Beauharnais left early," remarked the duchess a little anxiously.

"Yes, it is his turn of duty as aide de camp to the general."

Satisfied with Georgiana's answer, her mother turned her mind back to the events of the evening.

"Nothing could have been duller than Maria Yarmouth's ball! If she thinks she's checkmated me, she'll find that, when it comes to entertaining, she's more than met her match. I'm going to do something special, something no one has ever done before . . ."

A sudden cry of triumph told Georgiana that her mother had had one of her brilliant ideas.

"I ken what I'm going to do! I'll bring Neil Gow over from London and we'll have an evening of real Scottish dancing. You must teach Eugène to dance strathspeys and reels . . . you said we'd show the frogs how gay the Gordons can be. Well, we will!"

"Mama, please don't call the French 'frogs'—they're not at all like that when you get to know them. Of course, not everyone is as civil as they might be, but that is because many of the generals and so on whom we meet have made their way up from the ranks. To me, though, even they are always charming."

"And so I should hope, Georgy," said the duchess warmly. Secretly she was pleased that her daughter championed the French. It would be just as well that she liked them if things turned out as she hoped and Georgy became a Frenchwoman.

"Do you think they'd spare Neil Gow from Almack's?" Jane Gordon brushed aside Georgiana's doubt.

"Dinna' you worry, my love. Neil Gow's a Scot and he's aye keen on the bawbees. He'll like the sound of my golden guineas more than he'll care about offending those stuffy patronesses. They ken fine that Neil can do without them, but they canna' do without Neil. And I'll tell you what else I'll do." The duchess was now wholly in the grip of her project. "I'll have him compose a new strathspey for me and call it—why, of course, it must be called 'The Duchess of Gordon.' You leave it to Jenny of Monreith, my dearie, she still has a way with her."

So delighted was the duchess with herself that she even ceased to be annoyed that during the ball General Junot had scarcely left Lady Yarmouth's side. He, too, should learn how much more worthwhile was the duchess than the countess!

"Mama." Georgiana finally managed to make herself heard. "Have you forgotten that Eugène said he was going to give a ball?"

"Goddamn it, I did! Of course, I've no wish to outshine Eugène. But Maria Yarmouth's a horse of another color."

The duchess wrinkled her brow, but only for a moment.

"Eugène shall give his ball first and then I'll give mine. That will be all right, won't it, Georgy?"

"Yes, Mama, I think that's a good idea."

Yawning widely, the duchess made her way up to bed, bidding Georgiana an absent-minded good night because she was absorbed in her own thoughts.

"Before I give my ball we shall see what we shall see," she murmured to herself as her sleepy maid helped her off with her gown. "Since I am certain that Eugène intends to propose to Georgiana at his ball, it won't be necessary for me to give one, or to spend the money to bring Neil Gow over from London to Paris."

As she laid her head on her pillow, the duchess let her fancy roam even further ahead. Undoubtedly General and Madame Bonaparte would give a ball at the Tuileries in honor of their son's betrothal, and that would more than wipe Maria Yarmouth's eye, or anyone else's, General Junot's among them. The duchess fell into a contented sleep.

While Paris talked of nothing but Eugène de Beauharnais's ball at the house on which he was said to be spending millions, the Duchess of Gordon was in such high feather that she floated on air. She was unaware that Paris society derived much amusement from her hints, and her compatriots squirmed at the display she made of herself.

The duchess was ready to spare no expense to realize her darling dream of marrying Georgiana to Eugène, and she was determined that Georgy should have the best dress that money could buy. When the Gordon ladies drove up to Leroy's salon, every woman in Paris seemed to have the same idea. It was obvious that Eugène's would be the ball of the season, quite putting Madame Murat's quadrille in the shade.

"It's almost as splendid as the Tuileries," the duchess remarked loudly as she stared at the salon with its great mirrors, valuable bronzes, and glittering chandeliers. And well might Jane Gordon think so! Somewhere on Josephine de Beauharnais's giddy ascent to the peak of the social ladder, her path had crossed that of Leroy. While she rose to be the wife of the First Consul with an Imperial crown beckoning in the distance, he had become undisputed dictator of fashion. To be dressed by Leroy —which meant being able to pay his outrageous prices —was essential for any lady aspiring to be *à la mode*.

The duchess roamed around the salon, commenting on this and that until all the other ladies had left. Then she buttonholed Leroy imperiously and entered into a long discussion on the relative merits of blonde satin and worked lace. Georgiana took no part in this, but instead sat gazing pensively into the future, aware only of a fluttering of the heart as she thought of the ball. Eugène's warm glances, his pressure of her hand as he took it in the dance, his deference to her wishes and his desire to please her, were all clear indications of his feelings, but did she want him to declare them? Georgiana found herself unable to give an answer. Perhaps when the moment came—if it came—she would know what she wanted.

Chapter Six

"How different from last year at this time, when we were shivering with cold," remarked the duchess as the Gordon ladies set out for Eugène's ball. "I declare, it will be possible to sit out of doors."

Although it was only early May, the weather was pleasingly warm, the Tuileries gardens already brimming with flowers and the chestnut trees in the pretty little woods of the Champs Elysées bright with their red and white candles.

The duchess surveyed her daughter complacently. This evening Georgiana's beauty had an ethereal quality. Her dress of white-blonde worn over a satin underskirt of palest blue, with its high-waisted bodice, short puff sleeves, and graceful flowing skirt, suited her admirably. The duchess herself bloused over the corsage of her gown of blue brocade, which was richly worked in gold.

"Och," she exclaimed, "I'm the bluebell of Scotland but you, my love, are a white rose. I mind when Rabbie Burns visited us at Gordon Castle—bonnie Gordon Castle, he called it. He read us one of his poems, sweetly pretty it was. How did it go? Aye, I ken: 'Oh, my luv is like a red, red rose that's newly sprung in June . . .' If Rabbie Burns could see you now, Georgy, he'd surely change that red rose to white."

Impulsively Georgiana leaned to kiss her mother's cheek.

"You're very sweet to me, Mama. Indeed, I do love you."

The duchess wiped away a tear.

"Georgy, you're my youngest and favorite daughter. There is naething I wouldna' do for you. Remember that when ye are cross with me, as you sometimes are. At moments, my love, I get so tired of it all, politics and fashion and your father, and could wish myself Jenny of Monreith again . . ."

Jane Gordon bit back her words. Och, that loose tongue of hers! Georgiana must not be allowed to suspect that marriages were not always happy, even when a husband had been as much in love as Alexander had been.

"Of course," she hastened to say brightly, "to be an empress—that would be entirely different."

"It would indeed! I cannot imagine anything worse."

"Just you wait, my bairnie, and you will see!"

Georgiana almost choked with laughter.

"An empress? *I*? I'm never going to be an empress! It's far more likely that I should take to riding down Pall Mall on a pig!"

"Now, now, Georgy!" chided the duchess indulgently, pleased that the dear child did not realize how brilliant a future might lie ahead of her, although it really was not ambition that prompted her to further a marriage between Eugène and Georgiana. She truly believed that he would make Georgy a wonderful husband—and she was certain that for this evening he had purposely arranged a romantic setting in which to make his declaration.

As the Gordon carriage approached the Rue de Lille, Jane Gordon leaned over to whisper urgently to Georgiana, "Remember, my darling, whatever happens this evening, I want only that you should be happy—but I think you already know what will make *me* happy."

On the steps of his house Eugène de Beauharnais stood to welcome his guests, wearing the dress uniform of the consular guard, red breeches festooned with gold lace, a green jacket heavily frogged, his fur-edged dolman slung negligently over one shoulder, and under his arm the black fur busby with red busby bag and tall white plume.

He ran eagerly down the steps to kiss the duchess's hand and bend low over Georgiana's as he helped the ladies out of their carriage. Then he led them into the house, which was ablaze with lights.

"Should you not stay to receive your other guests?" asked Georgiana.

"I have already welcomed those I most care about," was the gay response, "and I want to show you over the house myself. I hope you will like it."

As they went from room to room, Eugène waved aside the ladies' praise of the elegance and luxury of the mahogany furniture, embellished with the Egyptian sphinx motifs in ormolu, which were the height of fashion.

"As yet you have seen nothing! Come!"

Eugène proferred his arm to the duchess, who refused it, saying airily, "I find it a little chilly. I think I will stay in the ballroom."

Feeling strangely shy, Georgiana took Eugène's arm as they stepped outdoors together.

"It is enchanting—an absolute fairyland," she marveled as she was led through the gardens. Candles were set within the hollowed-out fruit of hundreds of orange trees brought especially from the south of France. From a distance they appeared to be golden globes of light.

"No, no, you still have seen nothing!" Eugène repeated as they wandered on.

From the ballroom windows the duchess watched the couple disappear down a path. She quelled her impulse to follow Georgiana with a shawl.

"Far better for her to catch a chill than spoil such an idyll," she murmured to herself as across her mind flashed the memory of another young man in regimentals whom once—so long ago—she had met in the heather. With a sigh she turned away from the window and made for the card room. Soon, absorbed in a game of hazard, she became oblivious to everything else.

As Eugène and Georgiana strolled on they exchanged few words, but she was a little stirred by the pressure of his hand, now laid over hers. It was more compelling than those times when he had so often taken it in the dance. From the formal part of the garden they entered what seemed to be wild woodland, and Georgiana drew a little closer to Eugène, who laughed.

"You're not frightened of shadows, are you, Georgy?"

"N—no, not really frightened, but I thought I heard rustling in the bushes."

"A bird, perhaps, or a squirrel! See, I have my saber and will run through anyone who dares to attack you! But, you know," he added, suddenly serious, "at times one is frightened, very frightened, on the battlefield, and then one wants to run away, although one does not. I hope you don't want to run away from me, Georgy?"

"Of course not. I want to see all of your garden."

If that was not the answer for which he had hoped, Eugène gave no sign.

"And so you shall—this you call an English garden,

do you not? We call it a Chinese garden, why I do not know. I had it made in three days, for you."

Georgiana exclaimed in delight at the little stream cascading over stones and the profusion of spring flowers whose fragrance rose in the warm air.

"So this is what you said was even more beautiful . . ."

Eugene's dark head bent ever nearer Georgiana's blonde curls.

"No, we are not yet there."

Georgiana paused and drew in her breath with wonder as a small Greek temple came into view, its airy dome seeming to float on a circle of slender fluted columns. The flames of torches set between them flickered in the slight breeze. Gently Eugène drew her into the temple, where a silver mirror hung from the dome. Georgiana saw the reflection of her own face in it.

"This is the most beautiful thing in all my garden, Georgy—your face."

Too overcome to utter a word, Georgiana could only stretch out both her hands to Eugène. She made no attempt to draw them away as he covered them with kisses.

"Dearest Georgy, dare I ask the most beautiful thing in my garden to adorn it always? You must know that I love you, that I want you for my own. Will you consent to marry me and make Eugène de Beauharnais the happiest Frenchman alive?"

Neither of them now heard a rustling in the shadows as Eugène waited for Georgiana to speak. She could not utter a word. She had not needed the duchess's broad hints to tell her that Eugène had fallen in love with her, but, content to live in the moment, she had been reluctant to look ahead. Now that Eugène had declared his love, she was at a loss as to how to answer him. How far removed from the chill formality of Francis Bedford's proposal to her at Woburn was Eugène's tenderness and sincerity! In Georgiana's mind there was no doubt that he had proposed to her because he loved her, not because her mother had engineered an advantageous match.

"You say nothing, Georgy," Eugène said anxiously. "I am alarmed—but you must have guessed that I love you. Say but one little word to put me out of my misery. Is it my bad English you do not understand? Then I will say it to you in French—listen carefully. *Je t'adore et je veux que tu sois ma femme.* Now I will say it again, but this time in English, very slowly. Lady Georgiana Gordon, Lady Georgiana, Georgiana, Georgy—I adore you. Will you do me the great honor of becoming my wife?"

Although Georgiana's eyes filled with tears, she could not help smiling a little at Eugène's whimsy.

"You are so very sweet to me, Eugène, much too sweet."

But still she did not say the word he eagerly awaited. Why did she hesitate? She herself did not know.

"You do not answer me, Georgy. Ah, you are thinking of that other one, that English duke to whom you were affianced. I am jealous of him, very jealous."

Eugène looked so fierce that Georgiana shook her head violently.

"No, no, Eugène, I never think of him. I did not love him. It was my mother who wanted me to marry him. I was sorry that he died but so relieved that I was not obliged to marry him."

"Then it is someone else you love? Georgy, this is not possible. You would not—how do you say it?—play loose and fast with me."

"No, Eugène, I could not play fast and loose with you, nor with anyone as sincere and tender as you are."

"Then you will marry me, Georgy?"

Still Georgiana hesitated, willing herself to respond to so much love. Dear Eugène—surely no one was more deserving of it? Then what held her back? Deep in the recesses of her heart Georgiana knew, but it was a truth she refused to admit. *Banish the thought now and forever after!* Eugène wanted her and no one else did. With him she could be happy, and she certainly had no doubts that she could make him happy. Then why not do so?

"If you will have me—and you will teach me to love you—then I shall be honored to be your wife," she faltered, then for one fleeting moment wished her words unsaid but as Eugène took her in his arms he gave a boyish shout of delight. With the greatest gentleness, he kissed her lips and murmured endearments in her ear.

"I think that from the moment I first saw you in my mother's drawing room I loved you. Do you remember? And since then I have been your shadow. I shall always be your shadow, Georgiana, always be at your side to love and cherish you. You have made me so happy, so happy that I am ready to conquer the earth for you . . ."

Eugène bit his lip, hoping that Georgiana had not heard his unfortunate words. She was British, and, in spite of the peace, the British were the sworn enemies of France. Should war again break out—and the thought was never far from Eugène's stepfather's mind—then the war would be against England. Better not speak like a soldier and alarm his little English angel! They must marry as soon as possible, not only because of his ardent desire for her, but because if there were war she would be his enemy—something he could not bear to contemplate.

"You will marry me soon, Georgy, will you not?" he begged her urgently. "But first I must tell the general that I am lucky enough to have persuaded the most beautiful girl in France to marry me. I will go to him at once!"

"But, Eugène, you cannot leave your guests in the middle of your ball! Surely they must already be wondering where you are. Should we not return to the house?"

"Do you want to leave me so soon, Georgy?" Eugène asked sadly. "The only one of my guests about whom I care is in my arms, but, if it pleases you, we will return. I will take you into the ballroom by a back way, and no one will know that we have not been dancing the whole time. But *we* shall know, shall we not, Georgy, that in these precious minutes together we have taken the first steps into a future which will be ours."

Tenderly Eugène stooped and kissed Georgiana once again. Then, with a deep sigh, he took her hand, and together they stepped out of the little temple.

"You see, Georgy, that already I obey your slightest wish."

Hand in hand, Eugène and Georgiana made their way back to the house, but her hand in his was strangely cold.

After they had disappeared from view a shadowy figure emerged from the bushes to make its way through the undergrowth to the small gate which led to the Pont Royal and the Tuileries across the river. The figure scurried away into the darkness.

When Eugène and Georgiana slipped into the ballroom and he took her in his arms for a waltz, she glanced hastily about the room, but her mother was not to be seen. Of course; she would be playing hazard, and would stay in the card room until she had won or lost so much that she would be obliged to leave. When the duchess finally emerged it was immediately obvious to Georgiana that she had lost heavily. She was in a very bad temper, made worse by the fact that she had to wait for her carriage, because Damour was nowhere to be found.

To her daughter's great relief, the duchess grumbled about Damour all the way home. At this moment Georgiana felt unable to bear the inevitable transports of delight her mother would utter at the news she had for her. For a little longer she wished to keep her secret. There was something so genuine, so truly noble, about Eugène that she wanted to shield him from her mother's vulgar exuberance. Was this feeling that she cared more about him than about herself perhaps the beginning of love, Georgiana wondered. Tomorrow she would tell the duchess of Eugène's proposal, but tonight she wanted to be the only one to know.

Georgiana was in luck, because when they reached the Hôtel de Richelieu Damour was in the hall and she was able to slip away to her own room while the duchess vented her pent-up anger at him.

"You're drunk! Where have you been? When Lady Georgiana and I left Monsieur de Beauharnais's house you were nowhere to be found, and we had to return without you."

Damour goggled owlishly and sketched a few steps of the hornpipe, tripping over his feet. To regain his balance, he clutched at the duchess, who shook him off angrily.

"Lady—Lady—George-anna," he hiccuped, reeling from side to side, "going to marry M'sieu Beauharnais —always marrying someone, Lady Georgy."

"Damour, you're disgustingly drunk. Away wi' you to your own room at once, and when you've recovered yourself you'll give me an explanation of this regrettable lapse."

He swayed away into the servants' quarters, leaving the duchess to puzzle over his extraordinary behavior. In all the years he had spent in her service, he had always been a model of dignity and decorum. Suddenly the duchess realized that between Damour's misdemeanors and her own gambling losses she had overlooked the most important thing of all—Georgiana and Eugène. When she opened the door of her daughter's room, however, Georgiana appeared to be sound asleep. Drat the girl! Now Jane Gordon would have to wait until morning to know what had happened.

In the morning, a much chastened and hang-dog Damour first presented himself.

"Your Grace, I beg you to accept my humblest apologies. I am most truly contrite. Indeed, I am wholly at a loss to know what came over me."

"What *did* come over you?" was the stern question.

Damour cast down his eyes, fumbling for his words.

"Well . . . while Monsieur de Beauharnais's ball was in progress, and I knew that Your Grace would be among the last to leave, I slipped over to the Palais Royal to meet some friends. We sat down to play cards, and the next thing I remember is finding myself here on the steps of the *hôtel*." He hesitated. "I suspect that there is perhaps more to this than I know but please believe, Your Grace, that I shall be on my guard to see it does not occur again."

Although the duchess was intrigued by this dark hint, one remark had caught her ear to divert her attention.

"So you're a gambler, are you?" she asked curiously.

Damour held up a protesting hand.

"Oh, no, Your Grace, not a gambler just because occasionally I take a hand at cards."

If the duchess had not yet found out that he was as ardent a gambler as she was herself, then she could remain in ignorance!

"Then I insist you tell me, Damour, what are you? You've always been a man of mystery. Now, before I decide what to do about this deplorable incident, I think you should tell me the truth."

"There is little to tell, Your Grace. I know Your Grace

believes me to be a duke in disguise, even perhaps the Duc de Richelieu himself, but you are mistaken. Before the revolution I did know this house well, but in the servants' quarters, not the salons."

Damour seemed to fall into a dream, from which he was roused by the duchess.

"The Duc de Richelieu was my foster brother. We were brought up together by my parents in the country until he returned to Paris to be educated. As Your Grace will know, that was the fashion of the old régime. Armand and I were much attached to each other, and he did his best for me, but in those days little could be done unless one was of noble birth."

A bitter expression came over Damour's face.

"When Armand became duke he sent for me and had me taught many things and afterward I looked after his household for him. In private we were brothers but in public he was the duke and I the *maître d'hôtel*."

Even Jane Gordon, usually so insensitive to other people's feelings, realized how much Damour's pride had suffered. She made no further attempt to interrupt him.

"When Armand fled from the Terror I remained to safeguard his property, but because of my connection with him I myself was denounced. I had to leave in my turn when the *sans-culottes* were howling for *my* blood. Already the pikes were battering down the door, but I succeeded in making my escape through a secret exit."

As he thought of the bloody death he had so narrowly missed, Damour shuddered.

"Armand wanted me to join him in Russia, but by then I had reached England—oh, after many adventures—and entered Your Grace's household. I did not wish to leave." Damour bowed low. "I think Your Grace knows how devoted I had become to her and her family."

Another of the duchess's bubbles had burst. So Damour

was no nobleman, only a peasant! Still, she was glad to know the truth at last.

"And you wish to stay with me, I hope, and return to England, Damour?" she asked anxiously, his escapade apparently forgotten.

Before replying he waited for a long moment.

"Perhaps, Your Grace. I trust I am not being indiscreet, but if Lady Georgiana is to marry Monsieur de Beauharnais, might I not remain in her service? In this way I should still be with your family but also in my beloved Paris."

"How do you know Lady Georgiana is to marry Monsieur de Beauharnais?" asked the duchess sharply.

"Oh, Your Grace!" Damour smiled. "I have eyes in my head. Anyone can see that he is madly in love with her."

Although not wholly displeased that Eugène's feelings were so obvious, the duchess was a little uneasy when Damour went on, "Nothing else is talked about in all the servants' halls in Paris—and in the salons, too, I have no doubt."

"I do not mind *your* knowing, Damour, but I trust you have not spoken as yet to anyone else—of its being a certainty."

Damour threw up his hands in disclaimer and, thankful that the dreaded interview had ended so calmly, was bowing himself out of the salon when the duchess called him back.

"Ask Lady Georgiana to come to me here."

Even though the duchess seemed to have forgotten the previous night's incident, Damour himself had not. As he climbed up to Georgiana's room, he tenderly touched his still throbbing temples. This very peculiar headache was his only proof, but he was convinced that his drink had been tampered with. Well, he shrugged, if his tongue had run loose, what the duchess did not know would not worry her, and after all, an engagement between Eugène and Georgiana was common gossip.

A stony-faced duchess met Georgiana when she entered the drawing room.

"So, miss, it is from a servant I have to hear that you have engaged yourself to Monsieur de Beauharnais. Damour tells me that your betrothal is an accepted thing."

"I am indeed sorry, Mama, that the news should have reached you in this way, although how Damour knew I cannot hazard a guess. Eugène *did* propose to me last night at the ball, and I accepted him. I would have told you on the way home, but you were so angry that I couldn't get a word in edgewise."

Delirious with joy at the fulfilment of her hopes the duchess forgot her anger.

"Oh, my darling Georgy, so it is true! You will marry the Vicomte de Beauharnais! But he won't be a mere vicomte long—you'll be the Empress Georgiana, and that is better, far, far better, than being the Duchess of Bedford. I knew you were not the prettiest of my daughters for nothing!"

"Mama, please let us understand each other. I have accepted Eugène's offer because he is the most honest and sincere man I have ever met—his goodness shines out of his eyes. And he loves me, *me*, Georgiana Gordon, not the daughter of the Duke of Gordon. I wish I deserved to be loved as he loves me, but I shall try."

At once the duchess was up in arms.

"Nonsense, Georgiana. Of course you deserve to be loved. I knew Eugène fell in love with you the minute he set eyes on you."

"That's what he says, Mama," murmured Georgiana with a little smile.

"And everyone else saw it too! Fetch me my bonnet

—I must go and pay some calls and let everyone know . . ."

"No, no, Mama, you must not do so!" Georgiana exclaimed in alarm. "Eugène begged me to keep our engagement secret until he speaks to General Bonaparte. He has to choose his moment—it does not look favorable just at this time—the general has been in a bad humor lately. He has a great deal on his mind, Eugène says."

But all Georgiana's powers of persuasion were needed to make the duchess consent to keeping the engagement a secret.

"Lot of fuss about nothing," she grumbled. "What could the general have on his mind more important than his son's marriage? I thought the Corsicans had strong family feelings."

"I believe they do have, Mama, but surely you do not forget that the general is also the First Consul and that he has to govern France. That must come first."

This argument finally succeeded in silencing the duchess, although Georgiana herself had not the remotest knowledge of the general's functions, nor had Eugène made any attempt to enlighten her. In the few precious moments they had alone together when next they met, he was far more anxious to tell his beloved Georgy how much he adored her, how delicious she was, and how happy she made him than to worry her charming head with politics, especially the deepening crisis between England and France. Eugène himself knew that war was almost inevitable, but he had no wish to distress or alarm Georgiana.

"Every day that passes makes me love you more, Georgy—my little rosebud, my little English rosebud."

"But I'm not English, Eugène. I'm Scottish."

Helplessly Eugène wrinkled his brow.

"I do not understand the difference, and to me it is of

no importance. All that matters is that you are going to marry me."

"Have you spoken yet to General Bonaparte?" Georgiana ventured.

Eugène shook his head.

"Dearest Georgy, you may be sure that I shall seize the first opportunity of speaking to the general, because even you cannot guess how impatient I am for our marriage. Just now though, he is absorbed in political matters which need not trouble you. Come, my little Georgy, while I tell you again and again and yet again how much I adore you."

"Is Eugène coming to see you today?" was now the duchess's most frequent question, which as often as not drew the same answer

"I don't know, Mama. He sent word that, as it is a review day, he has to attend the general. If he can get away he will come, but you know how long the parades sometimes last."

"Och, Georgy," remonstrated the duchess, but without losing any of her good humor. "You should have told me that dear Eugène was on duty today and we could have gone to see the review. I must say, that magnificent uniform becomes him—he looks almost as gay as a Gordon Highlander."

And, to show that she was joking, the duchess poked Georgiana in the ribs and began to hum the song written about her:

> *There's a yellow thread in the Gordon plaid*
> *But it binds na' my love to me . . .*
> *For my love would 'list when a duchess kist . . .*

Georgiana was well aware of the duchess's pride in her song, and she naughtily interrupted her to gurgle,

"Eugène is going to grow a moustache! He says he looks too young to command men so much older than himself."

"There's certainly something very manly about military whiskers," recalled the duchess, "but they tickle, you know. Will you," she added slyly, "like being kissed by a man with a moustache, Georgy?"

To her mother's amusement, Georgiana blushed and turned her head away.

She doesn't even ask how I know, Jane Gordon thought cynically, since Alexander is clean-shaven. What an innocent little thing she is. Why, she might even be a faithful wife!

Georgiana's thoughts were all of her mother. She wished she would not continually probe into matters so delicate. No one could be more tender or more loving than Eugène, and she did indeed love him. But she had an uneasy feeling that her love was for a dear and kind friend, that the final spark was missing. Try as she would to give him her whole heart, always one tiny corner refused to yield.

"I wish that Eugène's military duties did not keep him so much occupied," she now sighed.

"Of course you do, Georgy," beamed the duchess approvingly, unaware that Georgiana was prompted by the hope if only Eugène could spend more time with her, the little block of ice in her heart would melt. Since his ball, however, the general was ever more demanding of his presence at the Tuileries. Argument was useless, because he always said, "Georgy, my little love, you know how much rather I would be with you, but the general comes first—he must be because he *is* the general! I am a soldier and I have to obey his orders, but if I am dutiful and submissive he will surely look kindly on my request for permission to marry you."

Eugène's twinkling eyes belied the seriousness of his

words. He could not doubt General Bonaparte's approval of his marriage. Where would he find a more delightful bride than Georgiana Gordon? True, she was English, but France was at peace with England, a peace he fervently hoped would last long enough for him to marry her.

"You are, of course, right, dear Eugène. Duty must always take the place of inclination. I am content to wait until you consider the moment favorable to speak to General Bonaparte," answered Georgiana.

Although she frequently doubted her mother's wisdom, Georgiana's confidence in Eugène was unbounded. Who, gazing into his handsome face with its open, frank expression, could think him other than a sterling character?

The duchess, less patient than her daughter, was becoming restive at the delay. Georgiana, surprisingly enough, succeeded in imposing her own will on her mother.

"Mama, we *must* wait on Eugène. He is far better acquainted with the general than we are—his moods, his temper. He is known to be difficult."

At once the duchess was up in arms for her new hero.

"Nonsense, Georgy, General Bonaparte is a very great man."

"That he may be, Mama, but because he *is* a great man we lesser people must study his wishes. We *must* allow Eugène to act as he thinks best."

To hide her annoyance, the duchess turned the tables on Georgiana.

"Then you two lovebirds should be more careful—you betray yourselves with every look and gesture."

But it was Jane Gordon herself who was betraying the secret engagement. Paris society, noting her new arrogance, drew its own conclusions, and was much amused to see her trying to bottle up her pride and joy and keep them from the world.

"I'm so happy, Georgy," remarked her mother, "that I made you sit for your portrait to Madame Vigée Lebrun. You remember how cross with me you were because you said you were so tired of sitting to Mr. Lawrence? Now you see that I was right to insist. I am *always* right, Georgy!"

Georgiana hid a smile.

"You know what I'll do? Eugène shall have your portrait for a wedding present."

"Thank you, Mama, on Eugène's behalf. I'm sure he'll be happy to have the portrait—he spoke of asking David to paint me."

Annoyed that she herself had not thought of having Georgiana's portrait done by General Bonaparte's favorite painter, the duchess waved this suggestion aside as being of no importance.

"How you teased me, you naughty girl, saying that I could not possibly want two portraits of you hanging at Gordon Castle and that at Buckingham House there was no room. Of course, what I really intended was that Vigée Lebrun's portrait should hang at Woburn Abbey."

Woburn Abbey? The duchess pulled herself up short. Both Woburn Abbey and the Duke of Bedford had gone clean out of her mind. Then a sudden thought struck her, and she wondered why it had not occurred to her before. Of course—John Russell was now Duke of Bedford and, although a widower, was a prize as great as his brother had been. Anyway, she thought comfortably, it did not signify now because Georgy was doing so much better for herself, or, rather, the duchess puffed herself up, because her mother had done so much better for her daughter.

It had been her idea to come to Paris, but even she had

scarcely dared to hope that Georgiana should have achieved this brilliant marriage. Eugène was everything she could wish for in a son-in-law, better than Richmond and Manchester and far better, of course, than that poor Robert Sinclair. How surprised and respectful Susan and Charlotte and Louisa and even poor Madelina would be when they heard of her triumph—and Alexander, naturally. He wouldn't like Georgy's living so far away from Scotland—nor, for that matter, would she herself—but then, she could always run over to Paris whenever she wanted to and Mr. Pitt could spare her. How rosy the future looked, the only fly in the ointment being Eugène's excessive caution. The duchess could not understand his hesitation in approaching General Bonaparte. She must speak to Georgiana again!

"No, Mama, definitely no!" said her daughter when the duchess mentioned the matter. "You must *not* tease Eugène! He knows what he is doing and I for one—and the most important one concerned, I am obliged to remind you—am quite content to wait."

"But, Georgy, I am so anxious to have everything settled—there is so much to decide, where you are to be married, for example, and it just occurs to me that Eugène is a Catholic. Oh dear, I never thought of that complication."

"Well, don't think of it now, Mama. These things work themselves out."

"Yes, perhaps," said the duchess doubtfully, "but maybe your papa . . ."

How irritating to be obliged to think again of Alexander! It would be disastrous if he should attempt to assert his authority. Perhaps, thought the duchess, she ought to write to him, or no, perhaps better not.

Indecision was not natural to Jane Gordon, but for once she found herself faced with a problem she could not resolve. Finally she decided that it would be far better to face her husband with a *fait accompli*. Once General Bonaparte's consent was assured, the duke would have to bow to the will of the most powerful man in France. She supposed disdainfully that even in remote Aberdeen Alexander had heard of Napoleon Bonaparte!

"Your Grace, a messenger from the First Consul asks if you will be good enough to receive him immediately."

As Damour made his solemn announcement, the duchess started up from her pleasant reverie. Hard on his heels entered one of General Bonaparte's aides-de-camp in full dress uniform with the aiguillettes of his rank. He made the duchess a formal bow.

"Madame la Duchesse, my master, the First Consul, bids me ask you to call on him at the Tuileries at four o'clock this afternoon. A carriage will be sent for you."

Before the duchess could recover from her astonishment or utter a word, the aide-de-camp had bowed himself ceremoniously out of the room. Jane Gordon sat perfectly still. General Bonaparte had invited her to a private interview! She brushed aside the form of the invitation, which had, of course, been an order rather than a polite request. That did not matter. What did matter was that Eugène must have now seen his stepfather and General Bonaparte most properly wished to give his formal consent to Georgiana's mother. A slow tear formed in the duchess's eye. What a marvelous climax to all her schemes and matchmaking!

"There, Georgy, what did I tell you? I knew that the general would give his consent, that he could not refuse anyone so ardently in love as Eugène."

"But, Mama, we do not yet know whether he has given his consent," was Georgiana's reasonable answer. "I should have thought that Eugène himself would have come or sent word to tell me that he had seen the general.

Perhaps there was no time. He must have seized on an unexpected opportunity."

"Of course the general has sent for me to give his consent!" exclaimed the duchess impatiently. "What other reason could he have? This is a very solemn moment."

The duchess's tone became prophetic as she gazed into a distant future.

"I like to fancy that it is not your happiness alone which is involved, important though that is. Think what lasting influence for good an English empress could have on England and France. Why, through your marriage to Eugène there could be peace between the two countries which would affect the whole world—Georgiana Gordon's marriage could alter the fate of nations!"

"Mama, you go too fast!"

In spite of herself, Georgiana was moved, but nevertheless she felt obliged to put a brake on her mother's fancies, only to find that nothing would stop her.

"How delighted dear Mr. Pitt will be with the news! I am sure that when your betrothal is announced the House of Commons will demand that he again become Prime Minister."

The duchess rustled over to her escritoire, then paused. No, she would write to Mr. Pitt on her return from the Tuileries, when she would have more to tell him about General Bonaparte. Lord Whitworth had better look to his laurels or he would find that the Duchess of Gordon made a better British ambassador than he did!

"Georgy, Georgy, I'm so verra' happy, so verra' happy!"

The duchess took a few dancing steps about the room as Georgiana watched in embarrassment.

"I must go and get ready for my interview with the master of France! Come upstairs, Georgy, and we will decide what I shall wear. It is so important that I make the best possible impression on the general."

Though less vocal, Georgiana's state of agitation was greater than her mother's. Now that the decisive moment had arrived, she did not know whether to feel glad or sorry. Surely she *must* feel glad that her future was now decided? And yet . . .

"I am fond of Eugène, certainly I am *fond* of him," she said to herself. "I admire all his good qualities, and I am sure he will make an excellent husband, but do I really deep down want him for *my* husband?"

"Georgy, Georgy, don't linger about. Come along!"

Georgiana did not, however, hasten her pace. If only Eugène would come and set her troubled mind to rest! Whenever he was with her she had no doubts; it was only when they were apart that this little nagging at her heart grew out of all proportion. She really did not know whether she welcomed or dreaded the general's consent, but once he had given it, the fact of her marriage to Eugène would be irrevocable.

"What do you think, Georgy? Shall I wear my yellow satin or do you think I should wear my new gown of tartan silk?"

The duchess's minute examination of her wardrobe, considering this dress and discarding that, obliged Georgiana to cease thinking of herself. She was simply relieved that her mother, wholly absorbed in the prospect of her tête-à-tête with Napoleon Bonaparte, had no time to spare for her daughter.

At last, when Georgiana and the duchess's women were worn out, the choice was made. She looked resplendent in her new tartan silk gown, her high bonnet crowned with nodding ostrich feathers of the same yellow threaded through the dark plaid, when Damour handed her into the closed carriage which drew up outside the Hôtel de Richelieu punctually at half past three.

As the coachman in the general's livery of bottle green and gold set his horses in motion, Jane Gordon leaned back against the squabs in the seventh heaven of happiness. Now and only now she spared a thought for her daughter. Georgiana might have shown herself a little more excited, but no doubt the child was overwhelmed. In any event, her excitement was unimportant. All that mattered was that it was set fair for one of the most brilliant marriages which had ever taken place— and it was all due to the Duchess of Gordon!

Chapter Seven

Sir Harry Featherstonehaugh yawned prodigiously, then yawned again. He was bored and quite unable to think of anything he wished to do. As soon as the idea crossed his mind of driving over to Brighton from his house at Uppark to join the Prince of Wale's party at the Royal Pavilion, it was dismissed. It was far too hot, and anyway, merely to think of the too familiar pleasures offered by Prinny made him yawn again.

Languidly Sir Harry wandered through his Stone Hall and the white and gold salon with its rich stucco ceiling and many portraits framed in white plasterwork, flanked by elaborate gilt sconces. Today he avoided looking at the likeness of himself painted while he was at Eton, that eager young face had no connection with his present mood. But in the red drawing room, he paused to look distastefully at Batoni's portrait, painted in Rome in the course of his Grand Tour—how many years ago? He grimaced as he realized with what speed they had slipped by. What a callow youth he had been, no more than twenty, when he succeeded to the baronetcy and ownership of Uppark, but at least in those days he had never been bored. He had wrung every drop to be distilled from his avid pursuit of pleasure.

Impatiently, Sir Harry retraced his steps to the dining room where once Emma Hart had danced on the table for his guests' amusement on one of the wild evenings when the Prince of Wales and his friends had descended on Uppark to indulge in uproarious junketing. Then Emma had captivated them all with her beauty and grace, as she had captivated him. Rarely did Sir Harry permit himself to think of Emma and the year she had lived under his protection at Uppark, but there were moments when thoughts of her obtruded. These were the times when his conscience troubled him that he had turned her out of the house when he learned that she was going to bear a child. He would swear now, though, as he had sworn then, that the child was not his but Charles Greville's, whose ideas of his host's hospitality extended to treating Sir Harry's mistress as an amenity offered to all guests at Uppark.

Yes, Harry Featherstonehaugh admitted to himself, he *had* treated Emma cruelly—after all, she had been little more than a child, a mere sixteen. It had really worked out to her advantage, however, since Charles Greville had passed her on to his uncle, Sir William Hamilton, and Emma Hart was now wife of the British ambassador to Naples, intimate friend of its queen, and the famous beauty who had enslaved Admiral Nelson, victor of the Battle of the Nile.

Sir Harry had wasted little time regretting Emma, and by now he had lost count of her successors, but as he strolled out onto his charming grounds the thought of her persisted. He was struck by a sudden idea. Emma was now in London, living with Nelson at Merton he had heard, and Sir Harry was aware of a faint feeling of curiosity to see what the years had done to her. He had been everywhere, seen everyone, done everything—why should he not go to London to pay a formal call on Lady Hamilton? Even if she shut her doors to him, that would at least be a new sensation.

When, a few days later, Sir Harry walked into Brooks's, he did not expect to find many of his friends at this season. He was particularly delighted to perceive his old schoolfellow John, Duke of Bedford, immersed in the *Gentleman's Magazine*.

"Well met, old fellow! What brings *you* to London? I had thought you were as rooted to Woburn as your crops."

Hearing himself addressed, John looked up, a warm smile lighting his face as he rose and grasped Sir Harry's hand.

"Harry! How pleased I am to see you! But I might ask you the same question. What makes you leave Uppark?"

"Boredom, John, boredom. I can think of nothing to do which would amuse me in the slightest. Am I getting old, John?"

"If you're getting old, Harry, then I must be also, as we entered Eton on the same day. But I don't feel at all old, and I am very far from being bored. Since Francis died there has been so much to do, all his work to carry on. You should really take up agricultural improvements, Harry. I assure you, there is never a moment to be bored when one is breeding sheep and cattle, trying out new methods of rearing crops and . . ."

"Spare me, John, please! You have known me long enough to know that such matters I leave to my agent. Embellishing my house and grounds, yes, but I have done so much that nothing more remains to be done. Uppark is a little jewel—oh, not on the scale of Woburn or Pet-worth, I grant you, but something more than a mere gentleman's residence."

Sir Harry planted himself more firmly in his armchair.

"Tell me something which will entertain me, John, now that I have been lucky enough to find you here. What's new in town?"

John's pleasant face clouded.

"The news is not good. I fear that Pitt was right when he warned the House of Commons that the Peace of Amiens was likely to prove a truce rather than a last-ing peace. In these stirring times you should not have given up your seat in the House, Harry!"

Harry Featherstonehaugh shrugged his shoulders.

"But you know I have little if any interest in politics, John. I merely took on my father's seat at Portsmouth because it seemed the thing to do, but those long sessions at the House with Burke and Sheridan and Fox and Pitt maundering on for hours were not for me."

"Silly old fellow!" said John affectionately. "Perhaps the Upper House is not so entertaining but, since I suc-ceeded, I make a point of attending whenever I am in town."

"You were always a better chap than I am. I have no pleasure in duty, and it is pleasure of which I am in search. I had it in mind to visit Emma."

"Emma?"

John looked puzzled, then his brow cleared.

"Surely you do not mean Lady Hamilton?"

Sir Harry laughed.

"Indeed I do, although to me she will always be Emma Hart. I have some curiosity to see whether she is the great beauty she promised to become when she lived with me at Uppark. She was only a slip of a girl then, but already dazzling. Sometimes I wonder why I let her go."

"I believe that she is indeed very beautiful, Harry, but you would be wasting your time. She and Nelson—Nelson perhaps more than she—are so besotted about each other that I doubt if she would even recognize you. No, no, Harry, leave Lady Hamilton alone. I have something better for you to do. Come with me to Paris!"

"To Paris, John?" Sir Harry shook his head. "No, I have no wish to go to Paris. I knew it well—we both did —in the old days. But so many of our friends have gone, some, poor wretches, to the guillotine, others scattered to the four corners of the world. Whenever I think of Chartres and how much he used to enjoy himself when he stayed with me at Uppark, I shudder. He was always the life and soul of the party. Who would have credited that he would become so rabid a revolutionary as to vote for the death of Louis XVI, his cousin to boot? No, John, Bonaparte's Paris is not for me. By the same token, whatever makes you want to go to Paris? I should not have thought you were the man to join the common herd rushing to see what Bonaparte has made of France."

John colored slightly before replying, with some hesitation.

"I told you just now, Harry, but you paid little attention. It seems likely that we shall soon be at war again with France. There is trouble about Malta and, as I read the situation, Bonaparte made peace only to prepare war."

"I still don't see why that should take *you* to Paris, John, unless, of course, you think you can persuade the First Consul to abandon his warlike plans?"

"No, Harry, I do not so flatter myself. I have another reason for going to Paris."

As John fell silent, Sir Harry looked at him curiously. John was such a steady fellow; he was unlikely to get any bees in his bonnet. Now, had it been himself! Sir

The Magnificent Duchess

Harry forgot his boredom and leaned forward to question John more closely.

"You're making a great mystery about this journey to Paris, my old friend. If you're not going to see the treasures Bonaparte has looted from Italy, if you are not going as, knowing you, I am sure you are not, to sample the pleasures of Paris, then why, since you insist that we are soon to be at war with France, do you undertake a journey there? Surely if you are correct the British will be moving out as fast as they can."

"That's just it."

Thoroughly aroused now, Sir Harry continued to drive John into a corner.

"If you do not stop being mysterious, John, I will call you out!"

"Oh, indeed, and for what reason?"

Sir Harry laughed.

"For tantalizing an old friend past bearing. Come now, come, tell me what is on your mind."

Speaking slowly, even reluctantly, John unburdened himself to his friend, relieved to have a sympathetic ear to which he could confide his anxieties.

"You know, Harry, that Francis was to marry Lady Georgiana Gordon, but he died before the wedding."

"Yes, I would have won a big bet that the Matchmaking Duchess would pull it off, but of course when Francis died the bet became null and void. Forgive me, John, I dare say it sounds heartless, but Mother Gordon is an irresistible target for gamblers like me. But I still don't see what this has to do with your going to Paris, or am I being very stupid?"

"Not stupid, Harry, impatient. Let me tell my story in my own way. Quite simply, the duchess and Lady Georgiana are in Paris, have been there now for months."

"Well," said Sir Harry reasonably, "supposing they are? If there is trouble, no doubt our ambassador—Whitworth, isn't it?—will take care of them. I assume that you have no connection now with the Gordons."

When John looked embarrassed, Sir Harry became increasingly puzzled until, with a great laugh, he burst out, "Don't tell me, John, that you are interested in Jane Gordon?" Then he clapped his hand to his head.

"What a fool I am—of course, it is Lady Georgiana, isn't it?"

"Yes, Harry, it is Lady Georgiana," said John, so quietly that Sir Harry felt rebuked. "I see I had better tell you the whole story—not that there is much to tell," he added heavily. "I saw her, Georgiana, for the first time at a ball given by Charlotte Richmond, and immediately felt drawn to her. My wife was still alive then, and it was wrong of me to allow myself even the slightest feeling for another woman. And from the beginning it was obvious that the duchess had set her sights on Francis, and I need scarcely tell you that when the Duchess of Gordon sets her sights on anybody he has little chance of escape! Not that to me it meant anything more than envy of my brother, because, in spite of myself, the more I saw of Georgiana the more attracted to her I was. Oh, I'll make no more bones about it—I fell in love with her, deeply and irrevocably. She is all I ever dreamed of in a woman."

A far-away look came into John's eyes as he paused for a moment before continuing his story.

"When Francis and Georgiana were betrothed I decided to leave Woburn, to go to Devonshire or Newton Stewart, it didn't matter where, so long as I did not have to stay at the Abbey to be tortured by seeing her the wife of someone else, even if it was my dearly loved brother. And then, God help me, my own wife Georgiana died. No one believed her to be so ill, because she was always malingering. Now I was free, but wretchedly free, because I felt in some sort responsible for my wife's death. I knew it was foolish, because her death made no difference. Georgiana Gordon was not free. Harry, I cannot tell you how miserable I was, but I loved Francis, and even if I could have done so I would never have tried to cut him out."

John dropped his head into his hands while all trace of laughter left Sir Harry's face.

"The worst of it was that I suspected that Georgiana was not happy." The muffled words sounded bitter. "But she was, and still is, entirely under her mother's thumb. And then, to my deep and abiding grief, Francis died."

"Well, John," said Sir Harry reasonably, "there was your chance. Why did you not take it?"

"Do you not see that I could not? For me it was bad enough to step into Francis's shoes, to take all his lands and titles. How could I take his bride as well? I may have been too scrupulous in observing the year of mourning, which has only just come to an end, may have been too fatalistic, adhered too closely to our family motto, *chè sarà sarà*, what will be will be. Perhaps I should have spoken up for myself, because at one time I was bold enough to fancy that Georgiana had a kindness for me, but you must realize how hopelessly entangled the situation was. First of all I was married, then she was betrothed to my brother, and how did I know how she would receive a declaration from me?"

"You were too timid, John, too fearful of rebuff."

"It may be that you are right." John smiled mirthlessly.

"Of course I am right, nor do I understand why you did not make an offer for Lady Georgiana, especially since you seem to think that she was not wholly indifferent to you."

"You may think me quixotic, Harry. You probably do, but to me it seemed to be a betrayal, an underhanded thing to do. I had believed that Francis was marrying from a sense of duty, because I was constantly urging him to do so for the family's sake. He was happy enough with Nancy Maynard, and he always laughed at me, until the Duchess of Gordon brought Lady Georgiana to the Abbey. Only after Francis died did I discover that he had offered for her because he, too, had fallen in love with her, because he *wished* to marry her."

"Your delicacy of feeling does you credit, John, but I cannot help but feel that you should have told Lady Georgiana of your attachment."

"My resolution did weaken," John confessed, "when I went to see her, to take her the lock of his hair which Francis left her. She looked so woebegone in the deep mourning she was wearing, and she seemed so overcome by Francis's thought of her that I could not at that moment obtrude myself . . ."

"Had I been in your place, John, been so violently in love with a girl, I should certainly have tried my luck. But you're not a gambler like me—you're too diffident, dear man, and think too little of yourself."

John shook his head.

"You're wrong, Harry—I'm by no means the plaster saint you imagine."

"That may be, but you do not look to me a happy man. I have no wish to be a Job's comforter but I must repeat that I think you were foolish not to make your feelings known."

"I might perhaps have done so had the duchess not dragged Lady Georgiana off to the continent. Of course, I do not hear directly, but people who have returned from France say that Lady Georgy is the reigning toast of Paris, and I have no doubt that the duchess is busy arranging a match for her, but God knows with whom. There are no English dukes to be had, and since the revolution French ones must be pretty thin on the ground."

"Wake up, John! No English dukes? Where are your wits, man? I see an English duke at no great distance from me, not unmarried, it is true, but a widower, which comes to the same thing."

"You mean me, Harry?" John's surprise was almost comical.

"Yes, you ass, I mean you. How long is it since Francis died? A year? No one can be expected to mourn for a fiancé forever, and nothing you have told me leads me to believe that Lady Georgiana is inconsolable for Francis. Aha, I see it, you rogue, you *are* going to Paris to try your luck."

"No, Harry, I am not! Despite all you say, I still cannot bring myself to believe that Georgiana would have me. What have I to recommend myself to so young and beautiful a girl?"

"I could tell you, but I will spare your blushes. What I *will* tell you is that you have a great deal to recommend yourself to the duchess: a ducal coronet, one of the greatest houses in the British Isles, as well as Newton Stewart and the Devonshire place, to say nothing of the Bedford estate in London and your rent roll. I say again, wake up, John!"

"I grant you all this, Harry, that although it means so little to me, it may be an attraction to the duchess, but I am far from believing that all my wealth and titles would influence Lady Georgiana. No, I am not going to Paris as you say, to lay my ducal coronet at her feet, but to bring her home."

John was now speaking with great earnestness.

"War may break out at any moment, and I hear on the best authority that Bonaparte hates the English, although he apparently has made them welcome in France. Remember that it was Nelson who destroyed the French fleet at the Nile, that it was Sidney Smith who checked Bonaparte's advance into India at Acre. Do you think with ten thousand English in his power—for I believe that there are that number in France at the present time—that he will let them go tamely?"

Although the library was empty except for himself and Sir Harry, John glanced about him and lowered his voice.

"Dundas tells me that the government has definite information that Bonaparte has prepared internment camps for his British visitors. Good God, can you imagine Lady Georgiana in an internment camp! I am convinced that, if war breaks out again, it will be fought to a finish between ourselves and the French, and that may take years! Harry, I am going to Paris to bring back the Duchess of Gordon and her daughter to England while there is yet time."

"And do you think you will be able to do so? I am skeptical that the duchess will tamely leave Paris because you tell her to do so?"

"Harry, I don't know," was the despondent answer, "but I should never forgive myself if I did not try, and for two reasons. The first you know, that I love Georgiana and cannot stand idly by when she might come to harm, and the second is because I know Francis would have wished me to do so."

"I agree with your first reason, John—indeed you have no need of any other—but I am in grave doubt as to your reception by the duchess. Jane Gordon, as you know, is not the most tractable of women."

All of a sudden Sir Harry Featherstonehaugh realized that he no longer felt bored but, on the contrary, full of energy and determination. Here at last was something to do! He even looked forward with relish to crossing swords with the Duchess of Gordon.

"John, I am coming with you! I know the duchess well, and of the two of us I think that I am the more likely one to persuade her to leave if she proves difficult, which I have no doubt she will. But I will come with you on one condition only, and that is that you make your feelings known to Lady Georgiana, and I'll wager—"

"No, Harry," John broke in, "don't wager on something which affects my whole future, my whole happiness. It is too sacred a thing. But I will accept gladly your offer to come with me. As soon as I saw you, I hoped that you would do so. If it comes to the crunch, two pistol arms are better than one!"

"Don't refine too much upon the dangers, John. It may yet prove to be a mere scare. When do you propose to set out?"

"Almost immediately, but if you are good enough to bear me company then I will wait for a few days. I do not wish to wait longer, for I do not believe that time is on our side."

Sir Harry rubbed his chin, and for a while remained deep in thought.

"I'll tell you what, John," he announced at last. "If you can give me a few days' grace, I'll post down to Brighton and see if I can extract some definite news from Prinny. I doubt if Downing Street or the Horse Guards would take me into their confidence, but the prince is a different matter."

Sir Harry rose from his chair.

"Grateful though I am to you, Harry, I do not feel I should interfere with your plans. Did you not say that you came to town with the intention of seeing Lady Hamilton?"

"So I did!" Sir Harry threw back his head and laughed. "I had forgotten all about it. No, let Emma enjoy her idyll with Nelson a little longer. After all, I can see her on our return. What I will do, while you make the preparations for our journey, is to pay a few calls here and there in town and also see the Prince of Wales. I have some friends who will give me the benefit of what they know. If, as you think, war proves to be imminent, we will make all speed to Paris."

Sir Harry broke in on John's thanks.

"It is I who should thank you—you've given me a new lease on life, and I, for one, shall enjoy a tussle with Mother Gordon."

At the library door Sir Harry turned to say with a smile, "And don't forget, I expect to be asked to be best man at your wedding, John."

Left alone, John smiled ruefully. What greater happiness could there be for him than to be married to Georgiana Gordon? But what would his welcome be when he arrived in Paris; what real chance did he have that she would accept him? Clearly Harry Featherstonehaugh thought poorly of him for not having put his fortunes to the test, but then it was unlikely that Harry could appreciate John's reasons for failing to declare himself.

Pleasant though it was to dream of Georgiana, there were many practical things to do. There was time for neither doubt nor hesitation. He must keep his mind firmly fixed on his primary object: getting the Gordons to leave France. Whatever else might happen was in the hands of the gods.

Sir Harry wore a graver face when, a few days later, the two friends met again at Brooks's.

"From all I have been able to glean here and there, John, it seems that your pessimism was justified and, that being the case, I am of the opinion that we should set out without delay."

From Dover the two friends made a smooth crossing in the packet in the excellent time of eight hours, but John's patience was sorely tried by the interminable three days spent on the journey from Calais to Paris. Since travelers were not permitted to bring their own horses into France, he had been obliged to leave his own good beasts at Dover, and the post horses he hired on the way were a poor exchange.

"Harry," announced John when they had taken their places in the duke's carriage, "I have taken a precaution I trust will be unnecessary, but, from what we both heard in London, it seemed a wise thing to do. I have hired an English vessel to stand offshore to be ready to take us off on our return—we may well arrive in a hurry."

"From the numbers of troops marching towards the coast, it does look as if your caution may be justified, John, although I cannot conceive that Bonaparte would be so foolish as to attempt an invasion of England. I must confess, however, that these troop movements do inspire me with a certain amount of alarm."

"Whatever may be their ultimate destination, they only confirm me, Harry, in my belief that I was absolutely right to come. From all the signs on the road there can, I fear, be little doubt that peace is not destined to last much longer."

But on their arrival in Paris the duke and Sir Harry seemed to be the only Englishmen who nourished any such fears, since the best hotel, the Hôtel de la Grange Batelière, was still crammed to the doors with foreign visitors. They actually experienced some difficulty in finding rooms for themselves.

"I take it, John, that you are going to call on the Duchess of Gordon immediately." It had not taken long to discover that the duchess was installed in the Hôtel de Richelieu.

John demurred.

"I believe that I should be well advised to call first at our embassy to hear what Whitworth has to say. If I can confront the duchess with some positive information, I should feel better armed to meet her. As you see, everyone here is quite unaware of any trouble pending."

Sir Harry laughed.

"John, John, you're a coward! If you're too much of a poltroon to face the duchess when you have come all this way with the sole object of seeing her, then I am quite brave enough. I suggest we go at once to the Hôtel de Richelieu. It is in the Marais—I visited there before the revolution."

But John insisted that he would go first to see Lord Whitworth. From the ambassador, however, he was able to glean little that was helpful.

"I am as much in the dark as you are, Duke," Lord Whitworth told John, who at this stage still withheld the real reason for his visit to Paris. "I can say only that, if you have come to see the sights, you should do so without delay, because the possibility of a sudden rupture of the peace does exist."

John thanked Lord Whitworth for his advice and returned thoughtfully to the hotel, where he found Sir Harry reading a newspaper.

"I believe, Harry, that we should be wrong to spread any alarm, since Whitworth believes that a rupture of the peace exists but that it is not imminent. We must proceed cautiously but not lose sight of the fact that, surprise being the most important element in attack, Bonaparte may spring one at any moment."

"While you were gone, John, I have been chatting to some fellows of my acquaintance whom I found here. It is perfectly clear to me that any warnings will not be attended to, since everyone shuts their ears to the possibility of trouble."

What Sir Harry did not repeat was that, in answer to his studiously casual inquiries about the Duchess of Gordon, he had been told of the rumored engagement between Georgiana and Eugène de Beauharnais. Only to himself did he say, "Poor John! If this should turn out to be the case, it will be a terrible blow."

Considering the circumstances, Sir Harry decided not to press for an early visit to the duchess, anxious to discover before they paid their call what truth there might be in the rumors. If he found them to be correct, he must try to shield his friend from the shock it undoubtedly would be to him.

"Well," he said gaily, "we had better pass ourselves off as model travelers and, as Whitworth advises, see the sights. We will begin by visiting the Louvre to inspect the treasures collected by Bonaparte."

The two friends set out on a conscientious tour of Paris, which aroused their unwilling admiration.

"I must concede," remarked Sir Harry, "that Bonaparte has made great changes since I was last here. The streets are cleaner and brighter, and he seems to be indulging in a veritable orgy of building."

But, hard though he tried, Sir Harry failed to arouse John's interest. He remained as indifferent to the splendid paintings and sculptures of the Louvre as to the magnificent salons of the fashionable rendezvous of Frascati's, remarking only that he had last seen the fabulous chandeliers in the palace of Versailles. More often than not John preferred to remain alone in the hotel with a book while Sir Harry went around and about, avowedly sightseeing, but in reality seeking news of the Duchess of Gordon. It was not long before he met Lady Yarmouth, only too eager to give vent to her spite against the duchess by detailing all the gossip.

"Jane Gordon is making herself absolutely ridiculous," she trilled. "She is the laughingstock of Paris with her tartans and her language and her gambling. I pity that poor girl of hers, really I do. So embarrassing for her to have such a vulgar mother. She seems a nice little thing, but to my mind lacks style."

With assumed indifference Sir Harry inquired, "Is there any truth in the rumor that Lady Georgiana is about to be affianced?"

"Oh, you do not need to be long in Paris," was Lady Yarmouth's spiteful answer, "to find out that the Match-making Duchess is at her old tricks! She is said to have hooked young de Beauharnais, but no one knows for sure. Although, judging by the way she puffs herself up, it may be true."

Everywhere Sir Harry went the same story was repeated, until he became convinced that John's only course was to visit the duchess and draw his own conclusions, especially as the success of his approach to Lady Georgiana seemed increasingly in doubt.

"John," he said decisively, "you have been on tenter-hooks long enough. Oh, don't think I have not observed how little interest you take in our expeditions. This very afternoon we will call on the duchess and her daughter."

John rewarded his friend with a grateful smile and a warm clasp of the hand as he rose from his seat with alacrity to order his carriage to be sent around to the hotel punctually at half past four.

Chapter Eight

With the duchess's departure at Bonaparte's summons, a great stillness settled on the Hôtel de Richelieu. Georgiana, too restless to settle down to anything while her whole future was at stake, pushed aside her tapestry, paced up and down the salon, and went over to the window to stare down into the little Place des Vosges, trying to imagine the meeting between her mother and General Bonaparte. Would Eugène be present? Again she wondered why she had not heard from him.

The duchess, impatient to set the crowning seal on her endeavors, found even the short drive to the Tuileries endless, but at last she was set down at the grand entrance, where a gentleman usher awaited her. He conducted her through the series of state rooms but the duchess was already familiar with these, and she was too agitated to pay further attention to their magnificence.

Despite her self-confidence, Jane Gordon was a little awed when they reached the First Consul's private apartments. She was aware that strangers were rarely admitted to his own study, the very heart of his dominion, but she reminded herself that *she* was about to stand to him in a more intimate relationship than anyone outside his immediate family.

At her entrance General Bonaparte's secretary rose from his desk in a window recess.

"Will you be good enough to take a seat, Madame la Duchesse? The First Consul will be here directly."

He gestured toward the window.

"I see that the troops are moving off the parade ground."

The secretary returned to his desk and again became immersed in his work as the duchess sat down on a small green sofa. She gave only a quick glance around the room, surprised to find it of such moderate size and lit only by a single window. Then she fixed her eyes expectantly on the door through which the general would enter. By the time she had waited for half an hour and still there was no sign of him, she could have made an accurate drawing of the study and its contents.

A magnificent bureau heavily chased with gilded bronze which rested on legs shaped like griffins almost dwarfed the room. In front of it stood an armchair upholstered in green kerseymere, its folds caught up with silken cords. Between the bookcases which lined the walls stood several marble-topped console tables littered with documents and maps.

When yet another quarter of an hour had passed and still the secretary wrote busily away and still the general did not appear, the duchess began to feel distinctly ruffled, and the little sofa on which she had spread out her skirts to show her tartan to its best advantage seemed uncomfortably hard. Even the First Consul of France should not keep the Duchess of Gordon waiting!

"Young man," she addressed the secretary imperiously, "I understood you to say that the First Consul would be here directly, but it seems to me that I have been waiting an unconscionable time for him."

"No doubt the First Consul has been detained, Madame la Duchesse."

Jane Gordon found this courteous but firm reply highly unsatisfactory. At least some expression of apology should have accompanied it, but too much was at stake to permit of anger or pique—she had already had many an experience with Napoleon Bonaparte's sharp comments.

Just as the duchess was once again about to speak harshly to the secretary, the door was flung open and the general entered at a rapid pace. He bowed jerkily to the duchess and tossed aside his black beaver hat and his gray greatcoat, worn over the blue uniform coat with white facings of the consular guard.

"Méneval, you can go."

The secretary bowed and slid silently out of the room through a door concealed in the wainscot as General Bonaparte took up his stance in front of the fireplace, in which a small fire was burning. He thrust his right hand between the buttons of his white kerseymere waistcoat and fixed the duchess with a penetrating stare, his dark blue eyes bright as molten metal.

"So, madame, I understand my son, Monsieur de Beauharnais, wishes to marry your daughter."

Heedless of the harsh tone, Jane Gordon turned on General Bonaparte the full force of a radiant smile.

"Yes, indeed, general. Is it not delightful? I have never seen two young people so much in love, but you must have observed for yourself how head over heels in love Eugène is, and my dear Georgiana is just the same."

"I have not seen my son, madame," was the curt rejoinder.

A little startled, the duchess wrinkled her brow.

"Not seen your son? Eugène told me that he was seeking an early opportunity to ask your permission to marry my daughter."

General Bonaparte smiled a cold little smile, so different from the look which occasionally lit his face. Then the smile was of such compelling charm that many men who had once seen it would cheerfully follow him through all hell to death, crying as they died, "Long live Bonaparte!"

"I have my own ways of getting information, madame. My son is a soldier and therefore brave, but it appears that as yet he lacks sufficient courage to address me on this matter. No, madame, I have a very efficient police, and you should instruct your servants to exercise greater discretion."

The duchess was taken aback. Who could have talked of a marriage between Eugène and Georgiana? Unless Damour on his drunken escapade had spilled the information among the crowd of pleasure seekers and pimps who haunted the Palais Royal, many known to be the First Consul's spies! Neither she nor Eugène nor Georgiana had suspected that a shadowy figure had lurked in the bushes around the little Greek temple in Eugène's Hôtel de Beauharnais.

Anyway, the duchess decided, the leakage was important only because of the general's annoyance that Eugène had not himself informed him of his plans. The general only needed calming down. Beaming affably, she leaned forward, and the yellow ostrich feathers on her bonnet nodded in time with the wagging finger she pointed at him.

"Ah, *you* know what it is to be in love, general. I do

not doubt that Eugène is walking on air and does not pay the same attention to practical matters as do people of our age."

Since Napoleon Bonaparte was no more than thirty, and young enough to be her son, this remark scarcely mollified him, but he ignored the duchess's tactlessness.

"Madame, love is for novelists and silly old women."

In spite of all her good intentions, Jane Gordon could not help bridling. She sat up stiffly on the sofa, hoping that the general had not intended an insult, but she immediately relaxed. He was far too great a man to stoop to such pettiness!

"You really believe, madame, that I will permit my son to marry the first young girl with whom he falls in love? Did I marry my first love? Did you?"

General Bonaparte gave a short laugh and withdrew his hand from his waistcoat to point a rude finger at the duchess, who stared open-mouthed. That Napoleon Bonaparte should have got wind of that early love affair of hers was surely impossible! If he had, then he must be the devil himself. No, he was merely provoking her. The general was well known to be a great tease! Of course, he had not married Désirée Clary, his first love, but the whole world knew how passionately he had fallen in love with Josephine de Beauharnais. Better, yes, far better, to ignore his innuendoes. The general was just playing with her, pretending to be opposed to the match only to appear magnanimous by yielding in the end. He was still speaking, and she decided she must give him her full attention.

"Madame la Duchesse de Gordon, I am already the most powerful man in France. Nothing can add to my power, but there is one further step I can take. The crown of France lies in the gutter, and I have but to pick it up on the point of my sword."

Napoleon Bonaparte thrust his face forward until it almost touched the duchess's; she recoiled as he added, with even greater emphasis, "Do you think that *your* daughter can aspire to marry the son of the man who will be emperor of France, the man who might himself one day be emperor in my stead?"

Rigid with shock at the general's attack, so far removed from the friendly reception she had so confidently expected, the duchess could find no words. No retort rose to her lips as Napoleon Bonaparte worked himself into one of his famous rages.

"My son, madame, will marry a princess and found a line of kings. The day is not far distant when all the sovereigns of Europe will plead to be admitted to my family. Do you think that I will permit Monsieur de Beauharnais to ally himself with the daughter of a petty English duke?"

As General Bonaparte fairly spat out his words the lock of hair on his forehead fell almost into his eyes, but he shook it back impatiently to glower at the duchess, now in a fury almost equal to his own. He gave her no opportunity to speak, however.

"No, madame, you can give your daughter this message from me—tell her to fix her sights a little lower, to curb her ambitions. The Vicomte Eugène de Beauharnais, adopted son of Napoleon Bonaparte, general of the armies and First Consul of France and soon to be its emperor"—beneath the white waistcoat his chest swelled almost visibly—"Monsieur de Beauharnais may seek a bride in any of the courts of Europe, which will be honored to give him the hand of any of their daughters. He has no need to look for a wife in the barbarous wastes of Scotland."

This was too much! Anger, disappointment, and hurt pride all fought for ascendancy in Jane Gordon. Shaking with emotion, she started off her sofa and marched up to the general, who had resumed his place by the fire. Now the words tumbled from her lips in a confused mixture of atrocious French and broad Scots.

"So, General Bonaparte," she stormed, "the daughter of the Duke of Gordon is not good enough for you and your adopted son. Whatever people may say, the Duke of Gordon could father sons and daughters, which is more than anyone can say for you! Why, everyone knows that you are incapable of fathering even a mouse! How dare you so insult the house of Gordon? I can tell you this, General Bonaparte! The Duke of Gordon's daughter may not be good enough for you, but one day my Gordon Highlanders may prove themselves *too* good for you! You haven't yet met *my* Gordon Highlanders in battle, have you, *General?*"

General Bonaparte understood little of the duchess's torrent of words, but he needed no interpreter for her face contorted with rage. How ugly she looked, and how vulgar! Moreover, she was daring to defy him! There were no bounds to English arrogance—look how they were attempting to trick him over Malta!

"So, Madame, if I understand you correctly, you have a puny little regiment to oppose to the great armies of France? But I am at peace with your country. Perhaps, like me, you have few illusions about the lasting quality of the Peace of Amiens? As if I were not aware that all your country wants is a mere breathing space to enable her to get a toe-hold on the continent of Europe so that her armies may meet mine, the invincible armies of Bonaparte. What audacity!"

The duchess was startled to hear a grim laugh.

"Let them come! They will be welcome! I shall deal with them as I dealt with the Italians and the Austrians and the Prussians, and your contemptible little regiment will languish in my prisons. Although, if they prefer, I will offer each man six feet of good French earth for his bones."

General Bonaparte was rudely pulled back to the present from this pleasurable prospect as he strained his ears to understand this woman's ravings. As if what she said mattered! He raised a hand to put a stop to the flow of angry words. Let her go—but he had one more thing to say to her first.

"Take care, madame! At this moment I have no friendly feelings toward your country—and there is ample room in my prisons for my unwelcome English guests as well as for her soldiers."

He picked up a small bell from a marble console and rang it violently. When his secretary emerged silently through the inner door he ordered coolly, "Méneval, show this . . . lady . . . to her carriage."

The duchess clenched her fists, obliged to exert every ounce of self-control to refrain from soundly boxing the ears of this insufferably cocksure little man. He already had turned his back on her and was studiously absorbed in the papers on his desk.

As she turned to follow Méneval out of the room, she launched her parting thrust.

"One day, General Bonaparte—and I promise you, that day will come—when on the field you meet the Fighting Ninety-second, *my* Gordon Highlanders, you will rue the day you treated the Duchess of Gordon and her daughter with so much contempt. *They* will avenge me, you little insignificant good-for-nothing chattering puppy!"

Trembling with rage, Jane Gordon swept out of Napoleon Bonaparte's presence, her silken skirts swishing with indignation and the plumes on her bonnet tossing in rhythm with the angry motion of her head. She flounced into the waiting carriage and threw herself back against the squabs, almost too angry to think, although she knew she must. What was she to tell Georgiana?

Sharply she ordered the coachman to moderate the pace of his horses. Before returning home to face Georgiana, so eagerly and confidently awaiting her, she *must* decide what to say to her. Another disappointment would surely send her into a decline! At this moment, Jane Gordon, stripped of all her affectations, was entirely given over to a mother's feelings. Setting her lips grimly, she there and then made up her mind. Georgiana *should* marry Eugène. How this marriage was to be brought about in face of the general's implacable opposition she did not yet know. Not for a moment did she believe that he would change his mind. She had seen in him a determination which equaled her own. A way must be found, but that was for the future. Her immediate problem was how to break the news to her daughter.

Jane Gordon knew herself to be a bad liar. However good her resolutions, whatever was on the tip of her tongue would tumble out. Already she could hear Georgiana saying when she confessed her defeat at the general's hands, "Mama, you can do nothing more! We must leave it to Eugène to try to make the general change his mind. I know, because he told me so, that his mother at least looks with a favorable eye on our betrothal."

The duchess had little confidence that where she had failed Eugène would succeed. If he had a fault it was that he was too easygoing. She could not mistake General Bonaparte's implacable refusal but, if she agreed with Georgiana, she would at least win some time. Unless, of course, Georgy should say, "I wish to bow out of the whole affair. Obviously I am fated not to marry."

By the time the carriage had stopped in front of the Hôtel de Richelieu and the groom had jumped down from the box to hand her out, the duchess had done some hard and rapid thinking. She had shaken off her depression and her natural optimism had reasserted itself. Now she almost welcomed the prospect of a battle with General Bonaparte. Let him find out which of the two of them was the better general. She had now resolved to fight him to the last ditch. She needed time for her campaign, but there was one thing to be done immediately to satisfy her thirst for action.

"Where is Damour?" she demanded of the lackey who opened the door to her.

"Monsieur Damour has gone out, nor did he say when he would return," replied the man, trembling at the duchess's angry face.

Jane Gordon had now convinced herself that Damour was responsible for leaking the information about Eugène and Georgiana to Bonaparte's police, and she intended to turn the full force of her displeasure on him, but she was frustrated by his absence. She paused with her foot on the stair. Was it because Damour had known what would be the result of her interview with the First Consul that he had taken himself out of her way? The duchess frowned. Could Damour himself be a police spy?

She had planned to go quietly to her own room before facing Georgiana, but the sound of voices as she passed the salon door made her change her mind. So much the better if there were callers! They would give her a respite before she need confess the truth. Perhaps, in the breathing space their presence gave her, she could concoct a plausible tale which would satisfy Georgy until she thought of something better.

The duchess composed her expression and entered the salon, to be greeted by two gentlemen who rose from their seats as she came in. To her amazement, she recog-

nized two old acquaintances in Sir Harry Featherstonehaugh and John, Duke of Bedford. Now what the devil
was John Bedford doing in Paris?

"My dear Duke, what good wind brings you to Paris?
And Sir Harry too! You are very wise—Paris is the
gayest city on earth. I cannot for the life of me see why
everyone does not come over from England to enjoy
themselves here. Am I not right, Georgy?"

"Yes, Mama, we are enjoying ourselves very much."

"Georgy is having a great success, you know," the
duchess gushed. "She took part in Madame Murat's quadrille and Monsieur Vestris considers her the best pupil
he ever had."

She turned to Sir Harry.

"And how did you leave Uppark? I have such happy
recollections of your parties there with the Prince of
Wales. Such a charming house and such delightful views."

Sir Harry bowed.

"I am particularly glad to see you," the duchess continued archly, "because you, I am sure, will do me a service. None of my acquaintance will escort me to the
Palais Royal, which I am dying to see—they say it is a
very Temple of Sin. I'm sure you, Sir Harry, will not
mind *that!*"

Sir Harry cast a comical glance at John, who gave no
sign of seeing it.

"I shall be very happy, Duchess, to escort you anywhere you wish."

"Excellent. Then we will arrange to go as soon as our
engagements permit. Of course, I do not intend to take
Lady Georgiana. The Palais Royal is no place for *her*."

"So I should think, Duchess, from what I saw on my
previous visits to Paris."

"Naturally, you know your way about, Sir Harry,"
said the duchess with a meaning look. "So much the
better!"

She turned to John to ask, with a point of condescension, "How is it that you found yourself able to leave the pigs at Woburn, Duke?"

John, who knew himself to be no favorite with the duchess, ignored the sneer.

"I found myself able to leave the pigs because I considered it of far greater importance to come to Paris. For a few weeks the pigs and sheep and the cows will, I have no doubt, get on very well without me. I have come to Paris, Duchess, to take you and Lady Georgiana home."

Sir Harry was consternated. John was taking his fences far too quickly and inviting the fall, which came immediately.

"To take us home? Have you got maggots in your brain, man? We have no intention of returning to London at this moment, or indeed, for a long time. We are very happy here, are we not, Georgy?"

"Yes, Mama," said Georgiana obediently in a still, small voice.

"You see," said the duchess triumphantly to John. "We are *both* very happy here."

She was struck by a sudden thought.

"And why have *you* come to take us home? When we do return, I can assure you we shall have no need of *your* escort," said the duchess rudely. "You, Sir Harry, I have no doubt have no such thoughts in your mind."

"I am sorry to disappoint you, Duchess. John is right."

Now that John had committed himself Sir Harry felt he had no alternative but to lend him his full support.

"We have come to Paris neither to see the sights nor to take part in its gaieties, although I shall, of course, be glad to squire you during our brief stay. John has told you why he is here and I am come to bear him company and give him such aid as I can."

The duchess turned back to John with rising impatience.

"What is all this nonsense, Duke? I can see no reason whatsoever for leaving Paris at this moment."

"Then, ma'am, in spite of all your political connections," John answered pointedly, "you cannot be aware that during the last few months relations between England and France have become increasingly strained."

The duchess smiled incredulously as John's tone became more serious still.

"Informed circles in England expect that we shall be imminently in a state of war again with France."

"That still doesn't explain why *you* are here," the duchess broke in. "I should have thought that if you were correct in your assumptions, you had been better employed in raising a regiment in Bedfordshire."

John cast a quick look at Georgiana, who was taking no part in the conversation. She sat silent, her head downcast but her color heightened, twisting her hands in her lap. The duchess, too, noted her agitation. Poor Georgy! No doubt she was wishing the duke and Sir Harry would go away so that she could hear the result of her mother's interview with General Bonaparte. Drat John Bedford! The sight of him had clearly aroused unhappy memories. Why did he have to appear when Georgy's heart was set on marriage to Eugène? Too bad that this moment she must be reminded of her earlier disappointment, especially when she might have to face another quite soon.

The awkward silence was broken by John's saying with some hesitation, "I cannot agree with you, ma'am, that it is not my concern. I consider it only natural that I should feel a sense of responsibility toward Lady Georgiana."

Again he cast her an oblique glance, but although she was intent on his words, she did not appear to be paying him any attention.

"When I last had the pleasure of meeting Lady Georgiana," John continued, "I ventured to express the hope that she would permit me to regard her as the sister she would have been to me had my brother but lived to marry her."

Georgiana looked up quickly, but John was facing the duchess squarely.

"I am only acting as my brother would have acted—as I am sure he would have wished me to act now on his behalf. I am aware that the Duke of Gordon is in Scotland and that your sons-in-law, ma'am, are busily occupied with their duties at home. As you say, only the pigs have any call on my time. Should the peace be broken abruptly, it may be difficult, hazardous even, for you and Lady Georgiana to leave Paris. To permit her to remain in a situation of danger would be a betrayal of Francis's trust in me."

"Hoity-toity!" snapped the duchess, seizing the opportunity to vent the anger which had been boiling ever since she had left General Bonaparte. John Bedford would be just as suitable a target as Damour—better perhaps. Throwing all discretion now to the winds, and intent only on crushing what she thought was John's unwarrantable interference in her affairs, Jane Gordon rushed on heedlessly.

"I am sure your feelings do you great credit, Duke, but I am at a loss to understand why you believe that Lady Georgiana stands in need of *your* protection. Your intervention is no doubt well-intentioned, but, I assure you, both unnecessary and officious."

To give greater effect to what she was going to say, the duchess paused. Then, assuming her most regal air, she announced with great complacency, "Lady Georgiana and I are under the best protection possible. She is to marry the Vicomte Eugène de Beauharnais, the son of General Bonaparte. So you see, Duke, that she has no need of the protection of any *stranger!*"

John winced at the emphasis put by the duchess on her last word, but she deigned to notice neither him nor Georgiana's look of agonized entreaty.

"You will be the first to congratulate my daughter, Duke, and you too, Sir Harry. I am this moment come from seeing General Bonaparte, who expressed his satisfaction with the betrothal and gave his consent in the most flattering terms."

There! The lie was out! Although the duchess was unable to resist throwing her triumph in John Bedford's face, even she had qualms when she remembered that later she would have to explain herself to her daughter, but she quickly justified her lie. Let not the Duke of Bedford think that because Georgiana had not married Francis she would not marry anyone! In any event, the betrothal of Eugène and Georgiana was a fact whether or not the general consented to their marriage.

John drew in his breath sharply and clenched his fist, only to let it drop in a gesture of despair. The duchess was an insufferable woman! From the bottom of his heart he pitied Georgiana for having such a mother, and, lest he betray his dislike and contempt, he avoided looking in her direction. Had he done so, he would have seen how Georgiana started at her mother's announcement and paled as her head dropped so low that her face was completely hidden.

Sir Harry quickly assessed the pent-up feelings which charged the atmosphere and with a polite smile and smooth speech gallantly spoke the words which at this moment John was unable to utter.

"We are indeed fortunate, Duchess, in being the first to congratulate you and Lady Georgiana on so notable a conquest. No one has anything but good to say of Monsieur de Beauharnais, and Lady Georgiana's charm and beauty speak for themselves."

He made an elegant bow in Georgiana's direction, but she was too confused to do more than murmur a few disjointed words to thank him for his congratulations.

While John gazed out of the window, Sir Harry, anxious to shield his friend against further distress, continued to chat with the duchess, until John squared his shoulders and again faced the room.

"Lady Georgiana, I trust you will accept my congratulations and best wishes for your health and happiness now and always. Come, Harry! We should not any longer detain the duchess and Lady Georgiana. I see, ma'am, my intervention was mistaken, but it was made from the best possible motives. Your servant, Duchess."

John formally bowed himself out of the room, but the duchess, who dreaded being left alone with her daughter, detained Sir Harry.

"It is agreed, then, that you will escort me to the Palais Royal?"

"I shall be charmed, ma'am. Unfortunately, I have not my own carriage with me as I came in Bedford's, so, if it does not inconvenience you, perhaps you would be good enough to send your carriage for me to my hotel, the Grange Batelière?"

"By all means, Sir Harry," was the gracious answer. "Does one good turn not deserve another?"

Since Sir Harry now seemed disinclined to stay any longer, the duchess, with a sinking heart, had perforce to let him go. Jane Gordon was left alone with her daughter.

"Is it true?" panted Georgiana almost before the door had closed behind Sir Harry. "I am really to marry Eugène?"

The duchess hesitated, then closed her lips in a firm line. Perhaps if John Bedford had not appeared at this crucial moment she would not have uttered her lie, but she had done so in an effort to protect Georgiana. John's visit must have reminded her of her previous unhappy experience. Francis's dying had been an act of God, beyond the duchess's control, but Napoleon Bonaparte's refusal of his consent to Georgiana's marriage was not. Fiercely the duchess told herself that she would do everything in her power before she tolerated his interference with her child's happiness. If necessary she would . . . she would kidnap Eugène! Not such a wild fancy, after all, since he could marry Georgiana at the British embassy. Fortified by this sudden revelation of a way out of her difficulties, the duchess was able to answer Georgiana's urgent question calmly.

"Yes, Georgy, my love, you are to marry Eugène."

"Oh!" The strangled sound broke from Georgiana, "I thought that—perhaps General Bonaparte might withhold his consent."

Whatever the consequences, the duchess was now determined to live out her lie, and if she could work out her plan perhaps it might not be one!

"Rubbish, you silly girl! What makes you imagine that? The general is delighted with the match."

Georgiana swallowed hard.

"That is wonderful, Mama. Somehow I did not think that he . . ." She did not finish her sentence, but said with a little difficulty, "Eugène will be so happy."

"But you feel happy, too, don't you, Georgy?" asked the duchess tenderly, herself acutely miserable.

"Of course, Mama, how can you ask?"

And Georgiana burst into tears.

On the pavement outside the house, John stood waiting for his friend, so lost in thought that Sir Harry had to speak to him twice before his presence was noticed. Then John said abruptly, "Take the carriage if you like, old fellow—I'm going to walk."

Gently he shook off the sympathetic hand Sir Harry

laid on his sleeve, but after a few paces he turned back to ask, "Do you believe that it is true, Harry—that she is going to marry de Beauharnais?"

"Even Mother Gordon would scarcely claim it to be so if it were not. And did she not say she had just come from seeing General Bonaparte and that he had given his consent? Jane Gordon may think herself the most powerful woman in England, but somehow I do not think that even she would dare to play ducks and drakes with the most powerful man in France."

John heaved a deep sigh.

"I suppose you must be right, Harry. I can quite understand that the young man has fallen in love with Lady Georgiana—nothing could be more natural."

Desperately Sir Harry sought some consoling words, but could find none. He could only look sadly after John's retreating figure as he plunged rapidly into the complex of narrow streets leading off the Place des Vosges.

When, some hours later, John returned to their hotel, he had acquired a semblance of calm and was so determinedly cheerful that Sir Harry found no opening to express his sympathy.

"Well," John said brightly, "we've seen all the sights in Paris except the greatest so before we leave we might as well take a close look at the Corsican. Whitworth has given me a card for a reception at the Tuileries tomorrow, so let us put on our best bib and tucker, Harry, and see the master of France while we may."

Sir Harry took the card John held out to him and read it aloud: " 'The Prefect of the Palace has the honor to present his compliments to His Grace the Duke of Bedford and Sir Harry Featherstonehaugh and to inform them that Madame Bonaparte will receive the foreign gentlemen who wish to be presented to her tomorrow at three o'clock.'

"By Jove, this might almost be a summons from the

king himself. There can be no doubt which way Bonaparte is going. I'll wager you that before the year is out
he'll be emperor!"

As John held up his hand Sir Harry laughed.

"Sorry, old man, I forgot you're no gambler. I'll have
to find someone else to take my wager, though no doubt
the odds will be so short I'll have difficulty in getting anyone to take me."

As next day the two friends proceeded through the
superb reception rooms of the Tuileries, admiring the
brilliant uniforms of the First Consul's entourage, Sir
Harry whispered to John, "He's a mean-looking little
fellow, yellow as a lemon. I am disappointed—I had
expected someone much more impressive."

"Whitworth tells me," John whispered in his turn,
"that he was thrown from his carriage while trying to
drive four horses at his country home at St. Cloud."

Soon it appeared that General Bonaparte's spirits were
as bruised as his body. When the two friends were presented to him by Lord Whitworth, he merely gave them a
curt nod before beginning to harangue the ambassador.
His tone of voice, his manner, and his gestures became
increasingly violent, until he reached such a pitch of
fury that it seemed he must fall into a fit.

"So you think I am preparing armaments against England in my ports?" he stormed. "This, I am told, is the
message your King George has sent to your parliament.
Oh, no, it is not I but you English with your pig-headed
obstinacy who are imperiling the truce. Are you already
tired of peace? Must Europe again be deluged with blood?
Is this what you wish?"

Standing near Lord Whitworth, the duke and Sir Harry
were greatly embarrassed by this attack but the ambassador heard the general out without letting any expression
cross his face. When at last Napoleon Bonaparte paused

for breath, Lord Whitworth merely bowed ceremoniously and moved away.

"I must say, I admire Whitworth's self-control," murmured Sir Harry. "Had Bonaparte addressed me thus, I must have struck him."

John paid little attention. His eyes were scanning the room.

"Be a good chap, Harry," he whispered finally, "and find out which of these good-looking young men is young de Beauharnais."

Sir Harry strolled nonchalantly over to the Duchess of Dorset, made her his bow, and stood chatting to her for a moment. She nodded in the direction of a group of young officers and, after a few moments of conversation, Sir Harry bowed once more and rejoined John.

"The tall dark-haired one in the dress uniform of the consular guard, red trousers, green jacket, very showy."

For a long moment John gazed intently at Eugène, then took Sir Harry's arm and led him away. As together they descended the grand staircase he said heavily, "Yes, he has everything to attract a woman: youth, good looks, charm. I could see all that, but I could also sense that he is a man of good character. Now that I have seen him, I feel happier. Lady Georgiana will be in good hands. He will make her a fine husband."

Sir Harry was silent. Nothing he could say would ease the pain in John's voice. To distract his thoughts, he pointed out the triumphal arch to the glory of the French army which General Bonaparte was raising on the Carrousel. Absorbed in his own gloomy ruminations, John barely gave it a glance, but suddenly roused himself to say, "Yes, there is evidence everywhere in Paris of the extent to which the Corsican is consolidating his power, but, Harry, we've just witnessed for ourselves how violent he can be. Do you believe that attack on Whitworth was unpremeditated? I do not. Bonaparte is clearly seeking a *casus belli*—and remember those troop movements we observed? It is vital that we impose some restraint on him or otherwise I foresee that he will make himself master not of France alone but of the whole of Europe."

John stopped dead, to continue, with the utmost earnestness, "Harry, I'm not leaving Lady Georgiana here. As like as not, Bonaparte would shut her up in one of his prisons out of pure spite, and I've small faith in the duchess's ability to cope with a crisis of *that* nature."

"But, surely," objected Sir Harry, "if Lady Georgiana is betrothed to young Beauharnais she can be in no danger. Did not the duchess say that Bonaparte had given his willing consent to the marriage?"

"I don't know. However confident the duchess may be, personally I distrust Bonaparte's intentions. If there is a rupture of the peace, he might well withdraw his consent to the marriage. After all, if he is at war with us, he cannot wish his adopted son to be married to an Englishwoman, and you've seen for yourself how obvious is his hatred of the English. Harry, you've accused me of hesitation, of timidity—well, I'm determined enough now. I'm going to take Lady Georgiana back to England, and if Beauharnais loves her, as he must—as anybody must," he murmured under his breath, "then he will follow her."

John's resolute decision came as a great relief to his friend. He had feared that John might yield to despair and return to England, trusting that with Eugène de Beauharnais Georgiana would be safe from any reprisals General Bonaparte might take against the thousands of English visitors in Paris. Sir Harry now let the subject drop and led the talk around to which theater they should visit that night and where they should dine.

"No doubt you remarked, as I did, John," he said later that night, when they were out of earshot of the crowds pouring out of the Théâtre Français, "how the audience cheered every reference to war."

"I did indeed, and it has made me more than ever anxious. I think it essential to go to the embassy tomorrow to have a word with Whitworth. He will tell us what we ought to do, but, even if he is optimistic, I am not, and my intention is to leave as soon as possible—the day after tomorrow, if need be."

"But how on earth do you think you are going to convince the duchess to leave?"

"I have no idea, but I shall find a way—I am determined to find a way."

"You may rely on me to do my best with her—you remember she insisted on my taking her to the Palais Royal. After all, she cannot suspect *my* motives. I may be a bachelor, but I am only a baronet and, beautiful though Uppark is, I cannot think it grandiose enough to tempt the Duchess of Gordon."

Chapter Nine

"How fortunate that you should have arrived in Paris just now," said the duchess affably as she took Sir Harry up in her carriage and gave her coachman the order to drive to the Palais Royal. "Everyone has been most disobliging about escorting me to the Temple of Sin. The French held up their hands in horror at the mere idea of my visiting it, and the British are even worse. There is a Colonel Everest whom I have befriended and invited to all my routs and balls, but do you think he would do me this little service in return? As if there were anything which could shock me!"

Sir Harry hid a smile. He had always found the Duchess of Gordon vastly entertaining, although others did not. Because of the dissolute company he had kept as a young man, he was no stranger to vulgarity, although the duchess's brand was peculiarly her own, since it was mingled with the hauteur of her rank and an impertinence which at times was almost royal.

"I am indeed happy to oblige you, Duchess, and I myself am curious to see what has become of the home of my old friend, Chartres. I knew it well in the old days."

As the carriage approached the Palais Royal the duchess carefully arranged the heavy veil she was wearing.

"There! Now no one can possibly guess who I am." She quite forgot that her tartan gown made her identity unmistakable.

"I want to see *everything*," Jane Gordon insisted as, leaning on Sir Harry's arm, she eagerly descended from the carriage. "And how I shall crow over all those milk-sops who profess themselves too pure to venture into these haunts of vice. I'll wager they do so in secret."

"I'll take you," said Sir Harry instantly. "What will you stake that we meet at least six of our acquaintance?"

The duchess thought for a moment.

"Is your Rockingham still standing at stud?"

"He fathered a promising foal last year in spite of his age."

"Good. Then five hundred guineas to Rockingham's next foal. I have a fancy to enter a horse in the Gimcrack Stakes, although I must enter it in Alexander's name."

"Done, ma'am. Six of our acquaintance, I say."

"And I say any number above six."

Laughing, they began to promenade the gardens, but soon Sir Harry was shaking his head.

"Perhaps I am getting old, but I cannot help contrasting this place as I knew it, when it was the most brilliant and elegant rendezvous in Paris, with all this riffraff here now."

"Riffraff" was perhaps too polite a word to describe the scenes of debauchery, depravity, and vice displayed before them.

"It is in truth an infernal sink of iniquity," remarked

Sir Harry not without a certain relish, as they proceeded on their way, gazing curiously into the tawdry booths which lined the promenade. Here the gourmand could eat his fill in a variety of gaudy taverns; there the ruined gamester might pledge his watch, his shoe buckles, even his coat before again plunging into the hopeless quest for a winning throw. Small playhouses offered doubtful puppet shows or dwarfs, giants, and every kind of freak. Quack doctors cried their wares, their strident voices competing with those of the vendors of licentious engravings, scurrilous libels, and erotic novels. All was offered with a knowing leer.

"Do you buy some of these brochures, Sir Harry," said the duchess negligently, adding with a chuckle, "and when you have read them you may pass them on to me."

As Sir Harry opened his purse, it was almost snatched from him by a ragged youth who quickly disappeared into the crowd, wholly indifferent to the baronet's loud cry.

"This place swarms with thieves and pickpockets, ma'am, I am told, so watch out for your reticule." Sir Harry lowered his voice. "And watch your tongue, too, because police spies are everywhere."

The duchess needed no reminder of this.

"I do not entirely understand how this place is laid out," she remarked. "Explain it to me, if you please."

"The gardens in which we are now walking are enclosed on two sides by the palace itself. Who lives there now I do not know. No one of any standing, I fancy, would wish to be a neighbor of these gardens as they are now."

Sir Harry shook off a daughter of joy bold enough to seize him by the arm. He was conscious as he did so, however, of a little regret. He would have liked to visit some of the private establishments which catered to every gluttonous and sensual appetite. He had heard of a salon where at a signal the ceiling opened to permit the descent of goddesses in the scantiest of classical attire. Of the existence of these salons he had no intention, however, of informing the duchess.

"As yet, ma'am," he remarked, "we are both losers. I have not seen anyone with whom I have the slightest acquaintance, but what I do observe is the domineering air of the soldiery. Look there!"

The duchess's eyes followed his pointing finger, to see everyone making room for an officer to pass, strutting and clanking his saber. The light of love on his arm laughed immoderately and chattered at the top of her voice to draw attention to her good fortune in having secured for herself so tall and lavishly bewhiskered an escort.

"They say," continued Sir Harry, "that the government makes a lot of money out of the gambling houses which it uses to finance the splendid new buildings Bonaparte is putting up all over Paris."

The duchess, however, was as unconcerned about the uses to which the government put the fruits gathered from exploiting people's vicious instincts as to the salacious remarks directed at her.

"*Hé, la belle,*" a voice called after her. "Show us the charms you're hiding under that veil."

"We have not seen any of the gambling saloons. These I *must* see," Jane Gordon urged Sir Harry, who hesitated, then shrugged his shoulders, knowing that she would not be gainsaid. He pushed a way for her through the groups of prostitutes in tawdry finery crowding around the doors, and they mounted the rickety stairs to an upper floor.

The duchess, her breath coming quicker as she heard the sweet sound of falling dice, advanced to the gaming tables like a man-o'-war in full sail, failing to notice a lady, like herself heavily veiled, who stood aside to let them pass.

"Good evening, Duchess! I scarcely expected to see you in such unsuitable surroundings."

Jane Gordon whirled around with a start, prepared to return the greeting, when, to her fury, she realized that the voice was that of Nancy Maynard.

"Unsuitable they may be for me, madam," she answered with cold disdain, "but no one could think them unsuitable for *you*."

By now Sir Harry, too, had recognized in Lady Maynard an old acquaintance, and prepared with cynical amusement to enjoy the scene which, knowing her, he was sure would ensue. He was not disappointed.

"About that there can be two opinions, ma'am. I hear you're still at your old game. Too bad that you lost your trick with Francis, wasn't it? So inconsiderate of him to die just when you'd tied the noose firmly around his neck!"

"Be that as it may," retorted the duchess, "he did one good thing before he died, and that was getting rid of you."

Nancy Maynard gave a sardonic laugh.

"So you really think Francis would have parted company with me forever? I could have told you to the day how long it would be before he thankfully returned to me! You cannot believe that that milk-and-water daughter of yours would hold him for long!"

"I'll thank you not to speak of my daughter."

"And why not, pray? Doesn't all Paris speak of her? You've won a great prize for her, haven't you, but you won't be able to carry it off any more than you were able to with Francis."

"Your sources of information seem remarkable," said the duchess grimly.

"And your servants highly indiscreet!"

This retort momentarily silenced the duchess. So it was Damour's indiscretion at the Palais Royal which had made its way to General Bonaparte!

Seeing that she had scored a point, Nancy Maynard continued in triumph, "You should teach your people to hold their tongues, but of course that is beyond you, since you can never hold your own tongue, can you?"

"That's enough from you, insolent creature," cried the duchess furiously. "With all these pimps and drabs, you're in your right element here. I have no doubt that you will end up as one of these old harridans who sell their bodies for a couple of sols."

"Do not, I beg you, be so concerned about my future," was Nancy's honeysweet reply. "Francis left me very well provided for—*he* knew what he owed to me. And I would remind you, Duchess, that I am Viscountess Maynard and can take my rightful place among all the peeresses."

The duchess was now in such a state of anger that she was at a loss for words, and Sir Harry thought it time to intervene. He had enjoyed the interchange hugely, but now he felt it should stop.

"Come, Nancy, as you *are* a peeress it is unbecoming in you to use language so intemperate. No doubt you and the duchess have your differences, but this is scarcely the place to air them, especially since there are eager ears to hear."

But the duchess had made a recovery and, ignoring Sir Harry, she launched another thrust at Nancy.

"Oh, I have no doubt you know where to lay your hand on money. General Bonaparte probably pays handsomely for information! And don't think you've heard the last of this. When I return to London I shall lodge the news in the proper quarter that My Lady Viscountess Maynard is a spy for Bonaparte—and you'll never dare show your face in England again."

Neither woman paid Sir Harry the slightest attention as he attempted to put a stop to an exchange charged with danger.

"I a spy!" shrieked Nancy. "You'll eat those words." She lunged at the duchess, clawing at her veil.

"Ladies, ladies! I implore you!" Greatly alarmed, Sir Harry put himself between them. "Remember, I beg, where you are—and who you are."

The duchess drew back, panting.

"I know who *she* is! A worn-out old drab—oh, yes, we all know Mrs. Horton—the Duke of Grafton's Mrs. Horton, the Duke of Dorset's Mrs. Horton, *everybody's* Mrs. Horton."

As Nancy prepared to make a fresh onslaught, Sir Harry seized Jane Gordon's arm and pushed her toward the staircase, followed by Nancy's shrieks of abuse. Once they reached the bottom of the stair, Sir Harry propelled the duchess rapidly toward the entrance of the Palais Royal, where her carriage was waiting.

"I think, ma'am," he said suavely as he handed her in, "that we'll call off our wager."

Too angry to pay him any heed, the duchess raged, "I'll go to Lord Whitworth tomorrow and have Nancy unmasked and thrown out of the country."

"I would not advise you to do so, Duchess," answered Sir Harry calmly. "Whitworth has a great deal on his mind at the moment, and to resolve a quarrel between ladies is the last thing he needs. Morning will, I am sure, bring better counsel."

But all the way back to the Hôtel de Richelieu the duchess continued to mutter to herself, her thanks to Sir

Harry merely perfunctory as she bade her coachman take him to his lodging.

"Whew," exclaimed Sir Harry as he collapsed into a chair when he found John quietly reading the *Moniteur*. "What an evening I've had! John, you do not know what you have been spared in losing the Duchess of Gordon as a mother-in-law. That woman is a virago!"

"You surprise me! What has the duchess been doing thus to earn your disapproval? I had thought you to be on good terms with her."

"And so I am. All was going well, and I managed successfully to distract her from the worst spectacles at the Palais Royal—incidentally, John, you should go to see it for yourself, it is truly unbelievable!—when by a horrid chance of all people we met Nancy Maynard, and which of the two was the greater spitfire I would not care to hazard."

"Nancy? Here? I can understand that between her and the duchess there can be little love lost. When Francis was betrothed to Lady Georgiana, he naturally gave Nancy her *congé*, which, as you may imagine, was not well received. He told me that in the end he had practically to use force to get her to leave Woburn."

"I am not surprised. I knew Nancy in the old days, when she was living with Dorset. Do you suppose, by the way, that the Duchess of Dorset receives her here?" Sir Harry sniggered.

But John was not listening.

"Do you think Nancy is in want?" he inquired seriously. "I know Francis provided handsomely for her, even more handsomely than she could have expected, but he was always most generous. He left her two thousand pounds a year—I do sincerely trust she is not gambling it away. In a curious way I feel a responsibility for her."

"You're an amazing fellow, John. Not many men would

feel responsible for their brother's discarded mistress."

John colored at Sir Harry's praise.

"Do you know how late it is?" he yawned. "I must go to bed, because I intend tomorrow to pay Whitworth another visit. Time is running on, and I am ever more strongly of the opinion that we should not linger."

Sir Harry was too tired, and had had too disturbed an evening to ask John once again how he thought he would persuade Jane Gordon to leave Paris. His friend had worries enough without his adding to them. Before he fell asleep Sir Harry's last thought was his hope to God that the duchess would not be so ill-advised as to complain to Whitworth about Nancy Maynard.

Early though it was next morning when John arrived at the British embassy, he found the anterooms full of English visitors all anxious to hear whether the ambassador counseled their departure. News of the scene created at the Tuileries by General Bonaparte had spread rapidly, creating great alarm among the English colony.

As John handed his card to a harassed secretary, another came out of the ambassador's room and called for silence.

"I am charged by the ambassador to tell you that his advice is that all those able to do so should leave Paris immediately. Any delay may result in a great difficulty in procuring sufficient horses."

Chattering excitedly, the crowd surged toward the doors to return to their lodgings, pack up their goods, pay their shot, and be on the road to the Channel ports with all possible speed. Only a few men and women were left in the anteroom who thought themselves of consequence enough to demand a personal interview with Lord Whitworth.

While John was hesitating over whether to go or stay, the secretary who had taken his card came up to him to say in a whisper, "His Excellency will undoubtedly wish to see you in person, My Lord Duke, but at the moment he is busily engaged in reading dispatches just arrived by courier from London. You will appreciate how occupied he is at this time, and I hope I am not wanting in politeness if I beg you to make your call a brief one."

John crossed one leg over the other and prepared to wait.

In his study Lord Whitworth was immersed in a dispatch marked "Private and Confidential," his brow wrinkling as he read the Foreign Secretary's opinion that feelings toward General Bonaparte in Britain were very unfavorable. On turning the page, he found the message ended on a more optimistic note:

> I am persuaded that Bonaparte will never venture to begin a war with us unless he can assume some popular ground which shall justify him in disturbing the general tranquility.

"I wish to God," grumbled Lord Whitworth to himself, "that Hawkesbury were here and then he would not write such nonsense. Perhaps when he reads my dispatch about Bonaparte's scandalous outburst he may begin to think differently. And, as if things weren't bad enough already, there is this infectious distemper prevalent in Paris—the influenza, no doubt. I hope to God I do not catch it!"

He rang a little bell on his desk and a secretary entered.

"Who is still waiting to see me?" he asked wearily.

"His Grace the Duke of Bedford, my lord, among others."

The ambassador's brow cleared.

"Oh, John Bedford is a sensible man. Show His Grace in. It will do me good to see someone who has his head on his shoulders."

"You know, my dear," Lord Whitworth observed to his wife that evening, "the Duke of Bedford conducts himself very properly. I wish I could say as much of many of our countrymen and women."

He sighed.

"In my short talk with him he showed me that *he* is perfectly aware of the character and projects of Bonaparte, not like some of the fools here who hero-worship him and fancy him as a friend of England because it suits their book to do so. But I wish I could think Bedford is too alarmist and exaggerates our danger. Although I am no admirer of the general, I find it hard to believe that he really desires to throw away all the advantages of peace. Well, we shall see."

Lord Whitworth leaned back in his chair. He had had a tiring and irritating day.

"One thing would certainly make my life here easier for as long as we remain. Bedford says it is his intention to take the Duchess of Gordon away from Paris, that this was his purpose in coming, but he hinted that she is so obstinate that she will refuse to go."

"Do not speak to me of Jane Gordon," cried the Duchess of Dorset. "That impossible woman! Her rudeness is matched only by her vulgarity. Did you not hear her the other night at the Foreign Minister's call out to Monsieur de Talleyrand, 'You are used to speaking in public. Will you call my carriage?' She's made herself the laughingstock of Paris society, but she's so foolish that she can't see that they have taken her up because they find her ridiculous."

"That may be so, my dear. I suppose you have heard that after General Junot fluttered for a while around that dovecot, he transferred his attentions to Lady Yarmouth, to the duchess's deep displeasure."

The Duchess of Dorset nodded.

"Yes, of course, I know, and so does everyone else in Paris."

"However much you dislike Jane Gordon," resumed Lord Whitworth after a pause, "you must recognize her genius when it comes to matchmaking. It is an open secret she's hooked Eugène de Beauharnais for her daughter, and *that* may be a prize far more worth having than a Duke of Bedford. Still," Lord Whitworth reflected, "Georgiana Gordon is a charming young woman, and no one can find a word to say against her. She always behaves very prettily and, I must say, she and de Beauharnais make a handsome pair."

"But do you think that General Bonaparte will allow them to marry?" interrupted his wife.

The ambassador shook his head.

"If he intends war, I cannot conceive it to be possible. That, by the way, is something we must watch closely. If in your social round, my dear, you hear of a rupture between Lady Georgiana and de Beauharnais, let me know immediately, because that will be a straw to show which way the wind blows. Not that I imagine that the match would please Bonaparte! He's certainly flying for higher game, but it is possible that Madame Bonaparte may try to win him over. Am I correct in saying that she appears to smile on the young couple?"

"You know Madame Bonaparte is so uniformly charming that it is hard to guess her real feelings, but I have heard that she does approve. Georgiana Gordon is such a sweet girl," said the Duchess of Dorset warmly, "that it would be a great pity if she were to be again disappointed. Unless she marries soon, I'm afraid, she'll be condemned for life to the society of that awful woman who bore her."

"My love," answered Lord Whitworth humorously, "you can scarcely expect General Napoleon Bonaparte,

First Consul of France, to take into account the feelings of a Lady Georgiana Gordon in determining his policy."

Indeed, even before the door had shut behind the Duchess of Gordon, General Bonaparte had dismissed from his mind the matter of Eugène's marriage. He had other, far more important things of which to think. The result of his deliberations was seen a few days later.

"Méneval," he called loudly, "bring me my big map of northern France with my troop concentrations marked on it."

After several hours spent poring over the map, General Bonaparte rose with a sigh of contentment and stretched himself.

"Well, Méneval," he said, tweaking his secretary's ear, and this was always a sign of his good humor, "my military preparations are as far advanced as I had hoped. All that now remains to be done is to make the final break with the British. Whitworth cannot be in much doubt as to my intentions. Send for Talleyrand, and let him be here within the hour."

While waiting for his foreign minister, the general paced up and down his study, his hands behind his back, pausing now and again to look out the window. When Monsieur de Talleyrand limped into the study, he wasted no time in greeting him.

"Talleyrand," he said shortly, "Lord Whitworth has repeatedly asked for his passports. See to it that he gets them—immediately. He must have been aware that his stay in Paris would not be long after that scene I made at the reception. By the way, I thought I did it rather well, don't you agree?"

As the general gave a short unpleasant laugh and struck an attitude copied from his favorite actor, Talma, Talleyrand bowed, hiding a look of long suffering. What a play-actor the general was, acting a play within a play!

"That's all! I have sent for Junot, who will make all the arrangements to clear the British out of Paris."

Talleyrand made a final ceremonious bow, but already the general had turned back to his maps. When the door opened to admit General Junot, Governor of Paris, however, he looked up and rose from his seat to take a stance in front of the fire.

"Junot, you must at once take measures to see that all the British in Paris between the ages of sixteen and sixty are arrested within twenty-four hours! Probably many of them have already scuttled away, but it is more than likely that, for lack of horses, they will fail to reach the ports. You will not find it hard to accommodate those left in Paris in my prisons until we can find somewhere else to house them."

The First Consul frowned. After a moment's silence he added, with greater emphasis, "You understand me, Junot? They must *all* be arrested, men and women. I make no exceptions. The British government must learn that little consideration can be awaited from their enemies if they break their faith given in solemn treaties."

General Junot saluted his old friend and was already halfway out of the First Consul's study when he was stopped by a peremptory order.

"This measure must be carried out by seven o'clock tomorrow evening. It is my wish that even the most wretched little theater or poorest tavern in Paris should not harbor an Englishman in its boxes or at its tables by eight o'clock tomorrow night."

Junot saluted again and made his way to the grand staircase at a pace far slower than he had taken when he had dashed to the general's study. His friendship with General Bonaparte dated back ten years, years during which he had learned the impossibility of arguing with him or questioning his orders. To imprison women and children, however, was the most distasteful duty he had yet been ordered to perform.

So long did Junot stand at the entrance to the Carrousel that an orderly came up to ask respectfully if he wanted anything. The general shook his head. What he wanted—but that the orderly could not do for him—was to make up his mind how to deal with the dilemma confronting him, the conflict between duty and inclination. He had many acquaintances among the English colony, had received them in his home and visited them in their own lodgings. Now it seemed he was obliged to turn traitor to those friendships.

At last Junot impetuously ran down the remaining stairs and jumped into his carriage. Later he would settle with his conscience as to whether or not he had disobeyed his orders but now he bade his coachman, "Drive to the Hôtel de Richelieu, and make haste."

Jane Gordon was astonished when Damour, in his most stately manner, announced, "Your Grace, General Junot asks if you will receive him immediately."

Junot? What could he want? Since Maria Yarmouth's arrival in Paris, his calls had been far less frequent. If he had at last found her so insipid that he wished to be reinstated in the duchess's good graces, he would have to show a considerable amount of repentance first, nor need he expect to be welcomed with open arms! Nevertheless, the duchess was titillated by the prospect of Junot's renewed attentions. Decidedly, things were looking up! With Sir Harry and now General Junot again in attendance, to say nothing of Colonel Everest (although of him she had seen little lately), she was assured of plenty of masculine company.

Another, even more satisfying thought struck Jane

Gordon. Junot was not only Governor of Paris and General Bonaparte's first aide-de-camp, he was also one of his oldest friends. Who then was a more likely candidate to bring her the general's apologies for his behavior, perhaps a message even to say that he had relented about Eugène's betrothal to Georgiana! Whatever the reason for this visit, her daughter's presence was superfluous.

"Georgy, you need not stay to see General Junot, you would only be bored. Run away and dream about Eugène."

As soon as Georgiana had left the salon, the duchess fluttered over to the mirror, gave a pat to her hair, and smoothed her gown before settling herself so regally in a bergère chair that it almost might have been a throne. She might no longer be slim young Jenny of Monreith, but her appearance could still please her.

"My dear General," she cooed, extending her hand, very much the great lady. Let him realize the difference between a Lady Yarmouth and a Duchess of Gordon!

Junot took the outstretched hand, kissed it lightly, then turned it over to implant a longer kiss on the duchess's palm.

"How I regret, my dear Duchess, that lately duty should have kept me from seeing you as often as I wished. You understand, I am sure, that the Governor of Paris has many calls on his time, time he would so much rather spend elsewhere—here, for instance."

The duchess smiled. Like a good soldier, Junot had got himself very prettily out of a tight corner, although not without some signs of embarrassment. She decided not to make his forgiveness too easy, but was surprised when he refused to sit down.

"I regret my absence all the more, madame, because duty now forces me to come on an errand both distressing and disagreeable."

If Junot's errand was unpleasant, then he was certainly not bringing an olive branch from General Bonaparte. What then was it?

Almost like a schoolboy, Junot stood first on one foot, then the other, twisting his shako in his hands, until at last, in a great hurry, he blurted out, "Alas, Madame la Duchesse, a state of war will soon be declared between your country and mine. The First Consul has ordered that all the British in Paris, irrespective of age or sex, are to be arrested. No doubt your government in London will do the same."

Junot bent forward earnestly and lowered his voice.

"In coming to warn you of this order, Madame la Duchesse, I have taken a grave personal risk because if General Bonaparte should hear of it I should be instantly dismissed from my post. Yet, in view of our friendship, I felt it impossible not to warn you so that you could leave Paris at once. The general has set a time limit of twenty-four hours on the execution of his order."

"Surely, General, you exaggerate," the duchess exclaimed, all coquetry forgotten.

"I wish, madame, that I did, but I have come directly from the general's cabinet, where he entrusted me with his most formal orders. I dare not delay longer because, as you can well realize, I have much to do, but one thing shall have my immediate attention. I will make it my personal responsibility to see that you receive your passports within the hour. I entreat you not to linger, but to leave Paris as soon as possible thereafter. I would advise you to begin your preparations for departure as soon as I have taken my leave."

Too stunned to utter a word, the duchess could only offer her hand feebly to Junot, who bade her farewell with obvious emotion.

"All I can add, madame, is to wish you a safe journey

home and to express the hope that in happier times we may again see you and your charming daughter in Paris. *Serviteur!*"

On the instant Junot was gone, leaving Jane Gordon in a state of turmoil, totally unable to credit the order of arrest. Surely, surely, to whomever else it applied, it could not apply to her, not to the Duchess of Gordon! She rose from her chair to pace feverishly about the room. Perhaps this order was part of General Bonaparte's war of nerves against her, a bluff even? But no, Junot had been too serious. When Jane Gordon was honest with herself, which this crisis forced her to be, she knew she stood too ill in General Bonaparte's graces to expect any quarter from him. She was still reluctant to believe, though, that when it came to the push he would dare arrest her.

The duchess ceased her pacing to throw her head back in defiance. Let him try to arrest her! Let him but try! Napoleon Bonaparte would learn of what stuff the Gordons were made! As for leaving Paris voluntarily, that was out of the question. She had come in the hope of finding an eligible husband for Georgiana, and in Eugène de Beauharnais she had found him. Why should she let him go? He was desperately in love with Georgy and, so far as she could judge—because the girl insisted on keeping her own counsel—she seemed to return his affection. At least she was ready and willing to marry Eugène, which was more than she had been with Francis. Of course, the duchess reminded herself, Francis was now an old story. If only John Bedford had not brought his brother to life again with the absurd fiction that he regarded Georgiana as his sister! A man's sister! She herself had as lief be a cold pudding!

Chapter Ten

Georgiana, sitting sadly in her own room, had reached the same conclusion. Far from dreaming of Eugène, as her mother had bidden her, she was trying to still the tumult in her mind. When John had made so unexpected an appearance, her heart had given a great leap and the truth which for months she had been resisting refused to be denied. It was John with whom she was in love, had been in love from the first moment she saw him. Now she admitted to herself why she had been unable to give her whole heart to Eugène. She loved him tenderly, but he just was not John! For a few ecstatic moments she had glowed with the thought that he had come to Paris for her sake, but that happiness was short-lived. John's demeanor had shown nothing of the lover, and Georgiana had been forced to accept the unbearable fact that he did indeed regard her only as a sister. Now she reminded herself that, even if he had come as a suitor, she could have done nothing. Her troth was plighted to Eugène. It was impossible to wound him so cruelly by casting him off, telling him she loved another man.

Georgiana leaned her burning forehead against the window, envying the carefree children whose mothers were calling them in from their play as dusk fell. In spite of her misery, a wan smile lit her face as she heard scratching on the door. Only Damour kept up the old practice of scratching instead of knocking.

"Come in, Mr. Damour," she called.

Damour entered with a conspiratorial air and closed the door firmly behind him before producing a letter from his pocket and handing it to her. For a moment she let it rest in her lap as she indulged the wild hope that it was from John—until she recognized the writing as Eugène's. She *must* put John out of her mind and hold fast to what he had said—that he had come to Paris only because he felt a sense of responsibility toward the girl who was to have married his brother. His astonishment, distress even, when the duchess had triumphantly announced her betrothal to Eugène could only be grief on his part that Francis was so soon forgotten.

Damour was hovering discreetly in the doorway.

"The messenger is waiting for an answer, Lady Georgy."

Georgiana opened the letter without curiosity. No doubt Eugène was writing to tell her that he was in attendance on General Bonaparte and unable to get away to see her. As she read, her brow darkened, and when she had finished the letter she turned back to the beginning to read it again, with even greater attention.

My adored Georgy,

I am at this moment come from an interview with the general—a very painful interview. He has informed me that, under no circumstances, will he permit me to marry you. His refusal is irrevocable. I have begged my mother to plead with him but I have little hope that she will prevail with him. In any event my mind is now made up. I still own some property in Martinique, my mother's birthplace, and if my darling Georgy will but deign to accompany me I will leave France and we will go together to the island.

Send me the word, my little dove, which I am awaiting so anxiously, that you will marry me as and where we can and that you will come to Martinique with your devoted

Eugène

An angry flush rose in Georgiana's cheeks as the letter fluttered from her hand to the floor. Why had her mother told her and told John so positively that General Bonaparte had given his consent to her marriage when it was a lie! What had the general really said to her? He could only have refused his consent, and the truth would obviously have emerged sooner or later. What had prompted Mama to make fools of them all? She determined to confront her mother, but first Eugène must have his answer. As Damour watched her anxiously and tried to read her expression, Georgiana walked deliberately over to her writing table and seized her pen to write the words which sealed her future.

My beloved Eugène,
I will do whatever you ask of me.
Georgy

When Eugène was ready to sacrifice his country, his brilliant career, his family, and everything dear to him, how could she hesitate? Her conscience would never rest

if she did so. She, too, would have to renounce her home
and family, but her sacrifice was small when compared
with Eugène's. It made her feel very humble that he
was prepared to count no cost because he loved her so
much. If anyone deserved the best of her, it was Eugène
de Beauharnais.

Damour sped away downstairs with her note, followed,
more slowly, by Georgiana.

"Why, Mama, did you tell me that General Bonaparte
had given his consent to my marriage with Eugène when
you knew it to be a lie?" she asked sternly as she closed
the drawing-room door behind her and faced her mother.
"I have just received a letter from Eugène in which he
tells me that, at the end of a stormy scene with the general, he categorically refused his consent."

The duchess looked profoundly embarrassed and fidg-
eted in her chair. General Junot's visit and the news he
brought had driven from her mind the realization that
Georgiana would eventually learn the truth from Eugène.
All she could do was to say airily, "Oh, my dear child,
you know the general's tantrums. When he saw me he
was in a bad humor because his horse had shied at the
music and put the cavalry out of step at the review. You
will see that he will change his mind when he has calmed
down."

The duchess's explanation did not ring true even to
herself, and she felt herself losing command of the situation as Georgiana remained so obviously unconvinced.
All of a sudden Georgy, the pliable young girl who had
always obeyed her mother without question, seemed
transformed into a woman who knew her own mind.

"The general will not alter his decision, Mama, and
you know it, but it no longer matters. Eugène has asked
me to go with him to Martinique, where he has some property. We shall be married before we leave, where and

when I do not yet know. I have given him my word that I shall go with him, and nothing and no one will persuade me to break it."

"Go to Martinique! Marry Eugène without General Bonaparte's consent? Have you run mad, Georgiana Gordon? I brought you to Paris to marry Eugène de Beauharnais, General Bonaparte's heir, the heir of the man who is to be emperor of the French." The duchess's voice rose shrilly. "Do you think I have been to all these pains and expense for you to marry a poor exile, a fugitive? To live on a wretched island far away in the Indies? Was this the brilliant marriage I contrived for you? It is one thing to marry the Vicomte Eugène de Beauharnais with fabulous prospects but quite another to tie yourself up with a miserable planter."

For two pins the duchess would have boxed Georgiana's ears.

"I forbid you to entertain this ridiculous notion."

"It is too late, Mama. So far you have always had your own way with me," Georgiana answered quietly. "Although you knew I did not care for Francis Bedford, you forced the betrothal to gratify your ambition to have four of your daughters duchesses. I grieve that Francis died, but you cannot conceive my relief at being spared *that* marriage. Then you wanted me to marry Eugène, and I consented to do so willingly. You cannot treat me as a plaything and a puppet to be made to move according to your whims. I can see now that it was not Eugène the man you wanted me to marry but a cardboard figure who might one day wear a cardboard crown. You were mistaken, Mama. It is the *man* Eugène who has honored me by falling in love with me, and if he wants to marry me, I shall not fail him. I will go with him wherever he chooses to go."

Before the duchess could recover her wits, Georgiana

had left the room. For once in her life Jane Gordon found herself utterly at a loss, her house of cards fallen about her ears. All these high-flown heroics of Georgiana's were stuff and nonsense. An unauthorized marriage would be worthless! What an unworldly simpleton Georgiana was! Bitterly the duchess realized that she who had seemed the most tractable of her daughters, had turned out to be the most obstinate—more so even than poor Madelina.

How to find a way out of this impossible tangle? Suddenly Jane Gordon smote her fists together. What was it Junot had said—Georgiana's sudden appearance had driven his visit clean out of her mind—wasn't it that the French were preparing to intern all the British who did not leave Paris immediately? Now, she didn't believe a word of it, but even if it turned out to be true, she didn't care, because at all costs she was determined to remain. Still, it was a useful bogey with which to frighten Georgiana. The girl must be brought to heel, but how? The duchess knocked her forehead. Of course! The first thing to be done was to prevent Eugène from making a breach between himself and General Bonaparte, and then they would put their heads together. Time was what she needed. She must have time.

"Call my carriage, Damour, and if Lady Georgiana wants to know where I am, tell her that I have gone to see Monsieur de Beauharnais."

That should give Georgiana pause! Suddenly the duchess recollected that she had not yet confronted Damour with the consequences of his loose tongue, still less forced him to confess whether or not he was one of Bonaparte's spies. She could not wait to do so now, and at any rate, further events had outstripped that folly. All that mattered was that she should be in time to prevent Eugène from taking any rash step.

At the Hôtel de Beauharnais, however, the duchess was informed that Monsieur le Vicomte was not at home, nor could his major-domo suggest where he might be found. Madame la Duchesse might try the Napoleon Barracks or the Tuileries, but even Jane Gordon did not feel equal to storming a barracks, and she had no confidence that she would even be admitted to the Tuileries. Baffled and furious, she returned to the Hôtel de Richelieu, determined to give her daughter a scolding she would not forget, but again she found herself baffled. Her request that Lady Georgiana be sent to her immediately was met by the answer that she was not in her room, and a search revealed her nowhere.

"Find her at once," was the duchess's peremptory command, but, while she fretted and fumed, no trace was found of Georgiana, nor had anyone seen her leave the house. Damour presented a bland face to all the duchess's fulminations, and he disclaimed all knowledge of her daughter's whereabouts. Adding to the duchess's irritation, at this moment he announced the Duke of Bedford. Why *must* that man put in his oar where it was not wanted?

John came straight to the point.

"Ma'am, I am come in all haste to beg of you to prepare for departure. It is now a matter of great urgency. I have it on excellent authority that Bonaparte intends to intern all the English still in Paris tomorrow evening."

"So General Junot has just informed me," interrupted the duchess, languidly. She ostentatiously stifled a yawn. Let John Bedford realize how important her connections were in Paris and not think himself the only one with confidential information!

The duke ignored the interruption.

"Lord Whitworth has already left and believe me, ma'am, that if we too do not leave immediately we shall find no horses. I am sending Harry Featherstonehaugh on ahead with my own carriage to ensure horses for our second stage, so I am obliged to beg a place in your carriage. It is imperative, Duchess, that you leave Paris within less than twenty-four hours."

John's words were spoken with such sternness that the duchess believed him capable of forcing her bodily into her traveling carriage. The shrewd Scot in her knew his advice to be sound, but the gambler in her was playing for time. Georgiana had unknowingly given her a trump card to play.

"Even, Duke, were I disposed to heed your warning, I could not do so. Lady Georgiana has disappeared."

"Disappeared? What do you mean, ma'am?"

"Exactly what I say, Duke. You know me to be a woman who speaks her mind plainly. Georgiana has disappeared and is not to be found. It is my belief that General Bonaparte has kidnapped her to prevent her marriage to his son."

John was thunderstruck, the more so since the duchess seemed quite complacent at the idea that her daughter had been abducted.

"You cannot be serious, ma'am! And did you not tell me that the general had given his approval to the marriage?"

Jane Gordon shrugged her shoulders with an air of nonchalance she was far from feeling.

"You know the general—or perhaps you do not—but he is a man of moods. Now the political situation has worsened, as you say, he may possibly have changed his mind."

Jane Gordon congratulated herself on what she thought was a neat escape from the trap of her own making, but John paid no heed to her, as his only concern was for Georgiana.

"Perhaps you refine too much upon Lady Georgiana's absence. She may have recollected some purchase she wished to make or . . ."

John stopped abruptly. He had been about to say, ". . . or perhaps she has a rendez-vous with Beauharnais."

He fell silent and then even the garrulous duchess had nothing to say. As an hour passed and then another and still Georgiana did not appear, they both became uneasy. Where could she be?

Georgiana was sitting in the little Greek temple in the garden of Eugène's house where he had proposed to her. She had scarcely returned to her own room from giving her ultimatum to her mother when Damour brought her another note from Eugène. In this anguished message he begged her to come to see him without delay.

When Georgiana asked Damour if it were possible for her to leave the house without being observed, his romantic soul was stirred.

"I will arrange it, Lady Georgy! There are many ways out of this house, as I know full well."

He at once took charge of the situation. First he ordered the carriage sent by Eugène to move off to the Rue des Francs Bourgeois so that if on her return the duchess learned that it had been sent he could truthfully say that it had gone away again. Then he led Georgiana stealthily down the back stairs to the servants' quarters and through a maze of winding stone passages until they reached a narrow and tortuous flight of steps into the cellars. Georgiana expressed her alarm that she would never be able to find her way back.

"Do not worry, Lady Georgy. It was this way that I escaped from the *sans-culottes.*"

After what seemed hours to Georgiana they came at last to a low door set almost invisibly in the wall.

Damour opened it with the large key he had been carrying, and he and Georgiana slipped through the door, to find themselves in the arcade on the Place des Vosges opposite the Hôtel de Richelieu. A few steps farther and they reached Eugène's carriage.

"Mr. Damour," begged Georgiana, "don't tell my mother where I have gone. She would not approve of my visiting Monsieur de Beauharnais, but he is in trouble and I must go."

"Rest assured, Lady Georgy, I will be silent as the grave."

The carriage drove rapidly away, and Damour watched until it was safely out of sight. He then returned to the house, satisfied to have got his own back at the duchess.

"Georgy, my darling, what am I to do?"

As she sat silent, looking up at Eugène, he paced up and down, his distress apparent in his expression and gestures.

"I am a soldier and I must obey my orders. The general has been too clever for us. He is the cleverest man in France—he knows everything! Almost immediately after I sent you my letter, asking you to come with me to Martinique, I received the general's orders to join my regiment without delay. And to ensure that those orders are carried out, he has sent one of his own aides-de-camp to escort me—call it arrest if you will."

Eugène raised his hands and let them drop in despair.

"I did not dare come to you, indeed I could not leave the house. Oh, my very dear one, what are we to do? I cannot dare hope that you will wait for me."

"Dear Eugène," said Georgiana softly, "if we cannot now go to Martinique, could you not give your escort the slip and come with us to England, or join me there later? You know that I would do my best to make you happy and forget what you have left behind. England is not so far from France as Martinique, you know."

Eugène smiled at her fondly and lightly touched her blonde curls.

"With you, my dearest Georgy, I should be happy anywhere, but I am a Frenchman and—it is very hard for me to say this to you—but to me England is always the enemy. You, too, *ma chérie*, are my enemy, my dear, dearest enemy."

Eugène fell to his knees, burying his head in Georgiana's lap. As she gently stroked his hair, she was nearer to loving him than ever before. She did love him, oh, indeed she did—she simply was not *in* love with him. If John had not come back so unexpectedly into her life, perhaps she might never have allowed herself to discover that it was he who occupied the secret place of her heart. But he *had* come back, and Georgiana knew beyond the shadow of a doubt that she would love him always. Understanding now the severity of the wounds love can inflict, her heart went out to Eugène. Greater than her duty was her wish to make him happy and spare him the heartache she herself was enduring.

As the sound of a military band was heard approaching from the distance, Eugène lifted his head to listen.

"Do you hear that music, Georgy? Do you know what they are playing?

"They are playing the *Chant du Départ*—the song of the men who march away. They are going to war, Georgy, as I must go to war, and the war to which we are going is against England. Perhaps not today nor tomorrow, but some day, somewhere, the French and British armies must meet on the field and fight the final duel between our two countries to a finish."

As if the music reminded him of his duty as a soldier, Eugène sprang to his feet.

"Georgy, that music is for me—my song of farewell. My darling, it is no good struggling against fate. I cannot hold you to your promise, much as I cherish you for having given it. You see"—Eugène's voice was very gentle—"that music speaks to me, stirs my blood. It speaks to me of battles, of gallant deeds to be done, and of glory—glory for France. You understand me, do you not, Georgy, you understand that I cannot help myself?"

"Dear Eugène, dear, dear Eugène, I understand you."

Now, as Georgiana took Eugène's hand, her thoughts were of him alone as he bent, tenderly kissed her hand, then folded her in his arms.

"Georgy, my Georgy, never, never shall I forget you. I can only hope that the hazards of war do not lead me to fight in person against your countrymen. When our two armies meet remember always that I shall be thinking of you and I myself shall never draw my sword against an Englishman."

With one final look around him, Eugène led Georgiana slowly and sadly away from the little temple.

"We were so happy here, were we not? Such a short time ago!"

Try as he would to recapture his normal gaiety, Eugène could not. The effort was too great. He could only say pathetically, "Do you know, Georgy, that during the revolution when they had guillotined my father and my mother was in prison I was apprenticed to a carpenter? Perhaps I would have been happier to remain a carpenter. Perhaps then my mother would never have married the general and everything would have been different!"

"But then, dear Eugène, we might never have met! But perhaps that too would have been better."

"No, no, Georgy, do not say so! Had I never met you I should never have lived. Before we part, my darling, there is one thing you must know—if I did not love you, I would not leave you. If I came with you to England I should dishonor myself, and how could I involve you in my dishonor? Even though my own heart breaks, I must honor my duty as a soldier of France."

They heard footsteps, and at the same time a discreet cough. Eugène and Georgiana pulled apart as a young officer approached, blushing as he did so. He saluted punctiliously.

"*Mon colonel*, General Déjean has arrived and asks that you be ready to accompany him forthwith."

The young man strode away toward the house while Eugène led Georgiana slowly through the shrubbery to the carriage waiting at the back entrance. He pressed one last fervent kiss on her hand, then stood at the salute until the carriage moved out of sight. He then returned to the house, looking to neither the right nor the left. A few minutes later he had mounted his horse and was spurring along the road with his escort on the way to the east.

Georgiana drove back to the Hôtel de Richelieu in a mist of tears. Eugène was a man any girl would have been proud to have as husband, and since she could not have the one on whom her heart was set, she would have been happy to marry him. Only Napoleon Bonaparte's grandiose ideas stood in the way. A sudden surge of hatred of the general rose in Georgiana, who was normally such a gentle girl. Her anger was not for what he had done to her but because of his cruelty to the adopted son of whom he professed to be so fond.

All at once she longed to be home, to be back in the dear familiar surroundings in Scotland with her father, who would not scheme and contrive for her but would allow her to follow her own bent. Surely henceforward she would make Gordon Castle her home, because who

now would want to marry Georgiana Gordon? They
would say that she brought only misfortune to those who
loved her. Had not Francis died and Eugène been torn
away from her? Now there was John, whom she loved
but who did not love her. Why, oh why, did it have to
be John? From the moment of their first meeting she
had been drawn to him by his quiet charm, by the gaiety
and fun which she had sensed lay beneath his sober
exterior and which she alone seemed able to draw out.
Why should one love one man and not another? Does one
ever know *why* one loves? To her own questions Georgiana could find no answers.

"Georgiana, where have you been?"

She had hoped to creep upstairs to her own room
unheard, but the duchess had been watching anxiously at
the window and seen the carriage draw up and drive
away.

"I have been to say good-bye to Eugène, Mama. Oh, do
not tease me, I am so unhappy! Eugène is all that is good
and kind. The general has ordered him to join his regiment in Strasbourg, and we shall never, never meet
again."

The duchess's bulk filled the doorway of the salon,
hiding John's presence from Georgiana but every word
she spoke stabbed him. He could not bear her to be so
unhappy. More than anything in the world, he wanted her
to have what she wanted, even if it dashed any faint
hopes he might once have cherished. But what was
there he could do for her? Only take her away from this
accursed country, even farther away from the man she
loved. Cruel it might be, but far crueller to leave her in
Paris to be the object of General Bonaparte's spite and
to be shut up in a place of internment, possibly for years.

"Nonsense, Georgy! Don't play the tragedy queen—of
course you and Eugène will meet again. Dry your eyes,

girl. If you could but see what you look like! You can safely leave the whole matter to your Mama. I myself will go to General Bonaparte."

The duchess, with no illusions now as to how the general would receive her, was well aware of the emptiness of this boast. He thought he had checkmated her, did he, by sending Eugène away! Well, he would see.

"Where did you say Eugène has gone, Georgy?"

With a sob Georgiana answered, "To Strasbourg, Mama."

John was increasingly uncomfortable, sure that, if Georgiana knew of his presence, she would not parade her grief in front of him, but his primary emotion was anger. He was furious with the duchess for buoying her daughter up with hopes she knew were false. She might not have noticed the man lounging under the arcades opposite, but he had, and he had also seen that, when the carriage with Georgiana had drawn up, the man had set off briskly in the direction of the Tuileries. Unless Jane Gordon was more careful, she would get heavily entangled in the web he suspected she was weaving. He had come to Paris to rescue Georgiana, and it was increasingly apparent to him that he should do so immediately, even though this involved taking the duchess as well. Why had he had ever professed to like her?

As he made his presence known, it was evident that Georgiana was dismayed to see him.

"Lord John—Duke—I did not know that you were here."

"No, Lady Georgiana. I am sorry. I should have shown myself before . . ."

Her woebegone face made him feel wretched, and he was loath to intrude on her misery, although necessity forced him to do so.

"I am sure that your wish at this moment is to be

alone, but my errand is too urgent to permit of postponement. You and your mother—indeed, all the English in
Paris—must leave without delay, under threat of impris-
onment or internment if they do not. I beg you most
earnestly, Lady Georgiana, to add your persuasions to
mine to urge your mother to accompany me and to
accept my protection to the coast."

"Thank you, Duke, I am grateful to you for having our
interests at heart."

Georgiana turned to the duchess and spoke with
authority.

"You hear what the duke says, Mama? We must go."

The Duchess of Gordon stared at her daughter in
disbelief. Never before had Georgiana spoken to her in
such a tone. Clearly she was shaking herself free of
the trammels her mother had taken such pains to weave
about her. This was a Georgiana whom she had never
imagined existed!

Chapter Eleven

For a moment the duchess was stunned; then she rallied, to lash out at her daughter.

"Don't you set yourself up against me, Georgiana! I have no intention of leaving Paris. As if General Bonaparte would dare to do anything to me—to the Duchess of Gordon!"

"Naturally you will do as you wish, Mama," was the firm reply, "but *I* am going with the duke. Eugène himself begged me to go home, and this may be the last thing I shall ever be able to do for him, to assure him of my safety."

This proof that Georgiana was wholly engrossed in Eugène de Beauharnais was bitter to John, but at this crucial moment there was no time to think of his own feelings. All his energy must be concentrated on convincing that impossible woman that she was not immune from the Corsican's anger, on the contrary, she seemed designed to be a special target. A deadlock seemed to have been reached, and John wracked his brains for something to stir the duchess out of her complacency. But Jane Gordon sat enthroned in her chair as if nothing would move her out of it, her face wreathed in a defiant smile, while Georgiana leaned her head on the chimney piece, staring mournfully into the empty grate.

The leaden silence was broken by the sudden eruption into the room of Colonel Everest, dressed for travel, booted and spurred, with his hat in his hand.

"Goodness! " exclaimed the duchess brightly. "So many callers! Anyone might think I was giving a rout party."

"Indeed, dear ma'am," guffawed the colonel, "that's just what it is! Boney has routed the lot of us, horse, foot, and artillery. The ambassador has already left, and the secretaries are busy burning documents and sealing up the embassy—I have just come from there. Grant and I are leaving immediately, making for the Swiss border. I came but to bid you farewell. My carriage is waiting below."

The duchess had a sudden inspiration. She turned to Georgiana, to ask coldly, "Where did you say Eugène had gone?"

"To Strasbourg," answered Georgiana without lifting her head.

"That's in the east, is it not?"

Jane Gordon's mind was now working swiftly. Why should she not take the road to Strasbourg and there let Georgiana marry Eugène? Once out of Paris, General Bonaparte would not know which way they had gone! That course would be an entirely different proposition from the Martinique folly. Josephine Bonaparte would surely cajole forgiveness for her son out of the general, who, faced with a *fait accompli*, would be obliged to reconcile himself to Eugène's marriage. It was a gamble but the duchess never hesitated to hazard all on the fall of the dice, however heavily it might be loaded against her.

Beaming affably on Colonel Everest, the duchess exerted all her charm.

"Almost, Colonel, you persuade me to accompany you. I have a great desire to see the Swiss mountains. Might I venture to beg your escort in leaving Paris, since the Duke of Bedford seems to think we might have some difficulty in so doing," she added, with a scathing look at John.

"Nothing would give me greater pleasure, ma'am, and believe me, it pains me to refuse." The colonel hummed and hawed uncomfortably. "But Grant and I are traveling very light—it would not suit Your Grace at all. I am sure His Grace of Bedford will see you safely wherever you want to go, and I shall look forward to waiting on you on your return to Buckingham House to satisfy myself that you and Lady Georgiana are safe and sound."

Briskly Colonel Everest bowed to the company, and in less than a minute had whisked himself thankfully out of the room.

"My God, what a narrow squeak!" he panted to Hilary Grant as he leaped into his carriage. "The Gorgon wanted me to escort her out of Paris and seemed to have some idea of going as far as Switzerland."

"I warned you, Thomas, not to say good-bye, that you would only meet some outrageous demand!"

"I must admit you were right, Hilary! But you know, when we return to England, the duchess may prove a most valuable social connection."

That was one Colonel Everest had lost for himself.

"He's in a mighty hurry," observed the duchess with deep displeasure, determined that when Colonel Everest presented himself at Buckingham House she would not be at home to him.

"And so, ma'am, should we be. There is not a moment to lose!"

"Rubbish, Duke! Stuff and nonsense, Duke! You cannot expect me to creep away like a thief in the night— nor have I yet said I will go with you! My clothes and Lady Georgiana's must be packed, and arrangements made about the house. A thousand and one things to be done, and *I* see no urgency . . ."

The duchess was merely making a strategic withdrawal from the position she had adopted because in fact her plan had matured. John and Sir Harry would see her and Georgiana safely out of Paris, where they would part company. She and Georgiana would then make for Strasbourg, although she had only the haziest idea of where it might be, but she could rely on Damour to find the way.

"No, ma'am." John controlled himself with difficulty. "I fear there is no time for all these refinements. Your friend sees the wisdom of traveling as light as possible. Believe me, I cannot too strongly stress that time is not on our side."

The duchess's damnable obstinacy was imperiling the safety of them all! He cared little for himself. He was thinking only of Georgiana.

"Your major-domo is a Frenchman, is he not? He can be at no risk from Bonaparte. Let him do what is necessary and follow us."

"What? Travel without Damour? I should not dream of it."

"I hope Sir Harry and I will prove adequate substitutes, ma'am," was John's dry retort. He was out of all patience with the duchess, but his anger was stilled when he stole another glance at Georgiana's woebegone face.

"Lady Georgy," John's tone was very gentle. "Can you

not impress upon your mother the seriousness of the situation?"

So pathetic was her answering smile that John could scarcely endure her pain. Involuntarily he put out a hand, then dropped it. He had no right!

"Mama, we are wasting valuable time. You know that the duke is right. I will ring for Damour."

As Georgiana made to pull the bell rope, the duchess glared and seized it from her. She was not used to being pushed into the background while Georgiana took command.

"No, *I* will ring for Damour," she snapped.

When he came, John and Georgiana held their breath. What new excuse would the duchess find for postponing their departure? To their immense relief as well as surprise, she said only, "Damour, His Grace, Lady Georgiana and I are leaving immediately"—there was a tiny pause—"for England. You will see to the packing up and locking the house, then you will follow us and meet us. But where?"

She turned to John, who hesitated. In his view, it was utter folly to arrange a rendezvous en route, which could lead to dangerous delays and complications, but he was too thankful that at last the duchess seemed willing to leave to raise any objections to her plan. Had he known what she really had in mind, his reaction would have been very different.

"I suggest Amiens, ma'am."

Damour's face fell, and he showed great distress.

"Of course it must be as Your Grace says, and I can only hope that General Bonaparte's malevolence towards the English does not extend to their servants. Your Grace is wise to be gone. You must know that for some time this house has been under surveillance. I did not wish to say anything about it for fear of distressing Your Grace."

The duchess shot a look of triumph at John! She actually took great pleasure in knowing that General Bonaparte considered her of sufficient importance to spy on her. Perversely, the information restored her good humor, but John had reached his breaking point. He now stepped forward and addressed himself with authority to Damour.

"Have Her Grace's woman and Lady Georgiana's pack what is necessary for their use on the road. If we are fortunate enough to obtain horses on the way, it should take us only three days to reach Calais. We will meet you two days from now at Amiens."

The duchess vouchsafed no word and, followed by Damour, she swept from the room. John and Georgiana were left alone.

"Thank you, Duke," whispered Georgiana as she prepared to follow her mother. "I knew you would stand our friend, our true friend."

John's friendship was sorely tried in the next few hours, because the duchess moved with exasperating slowness, giving and countermanding orders in her usual way. It was perilously near Bonaparte's deadline when she finally stepped into her carriage with many last-minute instructions to Damour.

"I am sorry to inconvenience you, ma'am," said John stiffly as he squeezed himself into a place among all the bulky packages, "but my man is sitting on the box. I would have sent him on ahead with Sir Harry, but I thought it advisable to have as many men with us as possible . . ."

"You surely cannot think that we shall be impeded in any way, Duke," scoffed the duchess. She was determined not to make life easy for John Bedford until Damour caught up with them. Then she would leave John to his own devices and head for Strasbourg.

"I am very sure we shall be, ma'am," answered John grimly as he ducked to avoid a parcel which threatened to fall on him. Impatiently he looked at his watch. "I only hope we may succeed in getting through the gates of Paris."

It was with a bare five minutes to spare that they did so by the fortunate coincidence that the duchess's liveries were of the same bottle green as General Bonaparte's and the guards passed the carriage through under the mistaken belief that it belonged to the First Consul.

As they swung northeast John heaved a long sigh of relief. The first hurdle had been successfully jumped, but he was anxious to put as many miles as possible between Paris and themselves. He could not shake off the suspicions aroused by the sight of Bonaparte's spy watching the Hôtel de Richelieu, and he was far from sharing the duchess's confidence that Bonaparte would do nothing to harm her. John believed that, on the contrary, he would make Jane Gordon the special target of his spite.

As if his anxieties and the difficulties of the journey were not enough, John's discomfort was increased by the duchess's disagreeableness. For Georgiana's sake he endured her inconsequential chatter and malicious gossip, groaning as he thought of the three days ahead. Never willingly would he have chosen Jane Gordon as a traveling companion!

"Of course you visited the Louvre, Duke, and saw the magnificent treasures brought back by the general from Italy, all those wonderful paintings and sculptures!"

"Loot, ma'am, stolen property."

"Come, come, Duke, are you not being rather hard on the general? After all, he is surely entitled to the spoils of war." And the duchess repeated the foolish remark she had made to Georgiana about wishing to see General Bonaparte in the British Isles.

"Then, ma'am," retorted John, goaded beyond endurance, "you would be doing your country a great disservice. The only place where I should like to see Bonaparte is safely incarcerated in the Tower of London!"

Deeply offended, the duchess lapsed into silence. In spite of his treatment of her, she still cherished a great admiration for Napoleon Bonaparte. John could relieve his feelings only by calling to his man from the carriage window to ask if they were being followed, which at least prevented the duchess from continuing her chatter.

John made no attempt to engage Georgiana in talk. Ever since they left Paris, she had said not a word. In fancy she was following Eugène to Strasbourg and wondering what would become of him. If the general did make himself emperor, would Eugène be chosen to succeed him, and would his stepfather insist on his making a brilliant match with a king's daughter? Georgiana now knew that, whatever the future held for Eugène, she would have no part in it. Had she any inkling of her mother's scheme, she would have vetoed it emphatically. Eugène's farewell had been final. In the conflict between duty and love, duty had won, and she respected and honored him for it.

Yet, the farther they drew away from Paris, the less Georgiana began to think about Eugène and the more about herself. Her own future looked bleak—an endless tussle with her mother as to whom she should marry. As she relived the past year she marveled at how much had happened to her. Except for bitter memories, she was precisely where she had been before. Could she, even a few days ago, have imagined herself sitting in a carriage with John Bedford on her way to England with another frustrated romance to her credit? When she ventured to peep at John, she saw his face was set in stern lines. Of what could *he* be thinking?

John's mind was, in fact, set wholly on the responsibility he had assumed of getting the Gordons away from Paris. With his usual humility, he wondered whether he had not taken too much on himself. Perhaps the duchess had been right that, if they had stayed in Paris, they would have come to no harm. But surely not—the evidence to the contrary was too strong.

The evening was still light, but darkness would have been welcome, because John feared that their headlong speed made them too conspicuous, a fear justified when, after three hours' driving, he saw his own carriage and Sir Harry pacing up and down outside a small inn, the Coq Chantant at Ecouen.

"Thank God you've come, John. I've had the deuce of a time with the postmaster here. His suspicions seem to have been aroused, how I do not know, but he swears all his horses are on the road, although I see he has some good cattle in his stables."

"How long have you been here, Harry?"

John had jumped down from the duchess's carriage, and was casting a critical eye over the horses attached to his own carriage and to the duchess's animals.

"A couple of hours or more."

"Then your beasts should be rested. They look well enough. We *must* press on and try to get another stage out of the duchess's horses but, Harry, do me a kindness. If I am obliged to travel with her any longer, we shall undoubtedly come to blows. Do you go with her and I will lead the way in my carriage. Follow me closely and do not, for God's sake, lose sight of me."

But before the change could be effected, a small troop of soldiers swept into sight and drew rein at the Coq Chantant when they saw the carriages. An officer swung himself down from the saddle and came up to John. He eyed him up and down before demanding, "Your passports, Monsieur."

After the officer had studied John's papers, he called Sir Harry over to inspect his. Still holding their passports, he jerked his head in inquiry toward the carriages, and the two friends' hearts sank.

"The ladies in the carriage are traveling under my escort," John said quickly, aware of the weakness of the statement. He cherished no hope that their rank would make any impression on this stern young man.

"All *Anglais*, hein? I have the First Consul's orders that all English are to be arrested and returned to Paris."

John and Sir Harry exchanged agonized glances, and John frowned when Sir Harry jingled the coins in his pocket. Clearly this young officer was not of the type to be bribed. While John was wildly casting about for some escape from the impasse, Sir Harry spoke up.

"The lady whom we are escorting is betrothed to Monsieur Eugène de Beauharnais, and we are conveying her to him, since he has left Paris to rejoin his regiment."

This was a lucky shot in the dark on Sir Harry's part, because John had had no opportunities to tell him all that occurred, since his friend had left Paris ahead of him.

The officer looked dubiously at the duchess, who had thrust her head through the carriage window. Despite his anxiety, Sir Harry could not resist a smile.

"No, that is not the lady—that is her mother."

Relief showed on the officer's face. He did not think that the popular young Colonel de Beauharnais would marry a woman years older than himself. Nevertheless, he hesitated.

"I do not know if you are speaking the truth, monsieur, because we have not been informed of the colonel's betrothal."

At this moment Georgiana's head appeared beside her

mother's. She was still so beautiful, despite her pallor, that the young officer drew in his breath sharply and made her an elegant bow.

"Ah, if that is the young lady, I understand. In the circumstances, I will permit you to proceed."

He gave a last admiring glance at Georgiana, handed the two men back their papers, bowed again, then quickly remounted his horse and, with a sharp order to his men, wheeled around in the direction of Paris. He soon was out of sight.

"Whew! " Sir Harry mopped his brow. "That was a near thing. Thank goodness for French gallantry!"

"Why in God's name did you say that, Harry?"

"But it's true, isn't it? That she's betrothed to Beauharnais?"

"It *was* true—I'll explain it all later. I wish to heaven for her sake that it was still true, but the young man *has* been sent to rejoin his regiment—you were right there, Harry—and the betrothal is at an end. You can imagine the Corsican's fury if he discovers that Lady Georgiana is passing herself off as his son's affianced bride."

"Well, it was lucky that I said the wrong thing, but it is obvious that we shall have to bluff our way through to the coast. All is fair in love and war."

When John took his place in his own carriage, his mind was busy with the hackneyed phrase which had rolled off Sir Harry's lips. All is fair in love and war— fair for whom? For Georgiana, for Eugène, for himself? Certainly not for himself. Georgiana was in love with Eugène and must now be suffering cruelly. Even if he had thought it fair to try his own luck, he had no prospect of success, and must reconcile himself to the bitter knowledge that he had lost her. John's future looked as black to him as the darkness ahead through which he was peering anxiously. Resolutely he put all other thoughts out of his mind but the urgent problem of getting them all to Calais. Even making the best speed possible, they must be three days on the road, and all depended on their being able to get fresh horses.

Much as John loathed sheltering under Eugène's wing, he now had to admit that Sir Harry's nimble wits had undoubtedly saved them. For himself, he would as lief be arrested or interned, but he had not himself alone to consider.

"How many miles have we gone from Ecouen?" he asked his coachman.

"About eight, Your Grace." He checked his horses for a moment and listened intently as the other carriage came laboring into view. "Her Grace's horses sound winded to me."

John frowned.

"Then we must risk pulling up at the next inn to which we come. The duchess and Lady Georgiana must be sorely in need of a little rest and refreshment. Drop to a walking pace so that her horses won't get too blown."

Sir Harry was not enjoying his ride in the duchess's carriage. Jane Gordon's mood had changed, and she kept up a steady monologue of scolding and recrimination, although neither he nor Georgiana made any attempt to answer her. At last the carriage stopped, and John put his head in through the window.

"Duchess, we are halting here. Allow me to assist you."

Ungraciously she allowed herself to be handed down, and gave an audible sniff.

"I should think so indeed! We have been traveling for an age, and I am as stiff as a poker. Och, my legs are quite shuggly."

As the duchess swept into the inn, Sir Harry could not forbear whispering to John.

"What a mother-in-law you've escaped! I've never met a greater tartar."

The inn was a poor place, but clean enough, and although the innkeeper was clearly unused to receiving such fashionable guests, he did produce some cold meats, although he had neither tea nor coffee for the ladies. Here at least, John was thankful to find, guineas spoke a universal language, but even guineas could not conjure up horses. No beds were available, but even had there been he would not have dared at this stage to make a long halt. To escape from the duchess's acid protests, John left the inn and patrolled up and down outside while the horses were rested for two hours. Sir Harry was obliged to bear Jane Gordon's lamentations alone.

Dawn was breaking when the horses were again set to and they were once more on their way. The road now showed up more clearly, and the carriage lamps were put out. Little but farm carts drawn by oxen met the travelers on their way, but at Beauvais the town was in a great stir.

John stopped his carriage on the outskirts and went over to the other carriage to confer with Sir Harry.

"I think it would be wise to avoid the main inn and see if we cannot get a change of horses in a smaller establishment where they are less likely to be watching for us."

"You think, then, that they are expecting us? There has been scarcely time for Bonaparte to be advised of our departure."

John shook his head.

"I'm not so sure, Harry. Don't forget that there was a man watching the Hôtel de Richelieu and also that when that young officer who stopped us at Ecouen reports meeting us, which he undoubtedly will, we stand a grave risk of being pursued and taken back to Paris."

But the duchess immediately vetoed John's suggestion that they find a small inn and stay only the minimum of time.

"Nonsense, Duke! You cannot expect me to go to any but the best inn. Lady Georgiana and I must wash and change our clothes. And look at you, unshaven and unkempt! This is not the way in which the Duchess of Gordon travels."

Stung to a retort, John could not help replying, "The Duchess of Gordon is not normally pursued by Bonaparte's police, but I will not argue with you, ma'am. We will do as you wish but remember if you please that you have been warned."

The coachman was bidden to drive to the Croix d'Or while John and Sir Harry each went his separate way, John in search of horses and Harry of news. When they met again, Sir Harry's face looked brighter.

"There is a rumor that Whitworth, who passed through here two days ago, is returning to Paris at Bonaparte's request. Apparently there is a great deal of confusion and uncertainty as to whether it will be peace or war."

"I fervently hope it will be peace, but for God's sake say nothing to the duchess. She will want to return to Paris at once, and we dare not give credence to mere rumors. My news is also better. I've been lucky enough to get hold of some horses—do not ask me how! It's the custom here to allow as many horses as there are people traveling, and I've managed to secure seven beasts. Four had better be harnessed to the duchess's carriage, and I'll drive tandem. With my lighter load, I shall keep up with you easily enough."

John was impatient to be gone, but the duchess had retired to a bedchamber and ignored the messages he kept sending her, each more urgent than the last. It was a full two hours after his return to the inn when she at last descended, having changed her traveling dress and with a fresh coiffure. John eyed her with disfavor.

As he was hustling her into the carriage, a company of gendarmes drew up outside the Croix d'Or with a jingle of harness and a clatter of arms. John cursed under his breath as their papers were brusquely demanded. Since it was too risky to use Sir Harry's stratagem again, the whole party, with the exception of the duchess, who was quite imperturbable, spent some agonizing moments. Fortunately, the officer commanding this troop proved more alert to the sound of coins chinking, and finally, after prolonged parleying and the surreptitious passing of a number of guineas, they were allowed to proceed.

As John had expected, the press of people and vehicles at Amiens (the halfway stage to Calais) was enormous, and an even deeper shade of anxiety clouded his face.

"I'm not going to risk a further rebuff from the duchess," he told Harry. "We'll go directly to the Lion d'Argent, which is the best inn in the town."

Sir Harry agreed, saying with a laugh, "Do you know, John, I cannot imagine why I was bored at Uppark! Once I get home, believe me, peace and a quiet life will be welcome. Oh, to be relieved of the sound of Jane Gordon's cackle."

"Indeed, Harry," said John seriously, "I feel guilty to have embroiled you in all this trouble."

"Then stop feeling guilty, because I have enjoyed myself hugely. It is an experience I would not have missed—providing, of course, that we succeed in escaping from Bonaparte's clutches, but this I am confident we shall do."

Sir Harry's confidence was, however, slightly diminished when he and John were hailed by a dusty and mud-spattered horseman.

"Good God, it is Damour, is it not?" cried John. "How did you succeed in getting here so soon?"

Damour dismounted stiffly and, holding the bridle of his horse, he embarked on his story.

"You had not been gone above an hour, Your Grace, when two of Bonaparte's police came to the house with a warrant of arrest. They searched it from top to bottom, furious that Her Grace had eluded them. They proceeded to haul me off to the collection area for British prisoners—for I must tell Your Grace that Bonaparte was as good as his word. All the English remaining in Paris at seven o'clock that evening were arrested. By great good fortune I succeeded in giving the *policiers* the slip, as I had done with the *sans-culottes*, and got away to keep my rendezvous with Her Grace."

The duchess welcomed Damour with cries of joy, which turned to lamentations when she found that all her baggage had been left behind. Georgiana pulled her up sharply.

"Oh, Mama, what do a few ball gowns signify? You must now realize how right the duke was to urge our departure."

Ignoring Georgiana, the duchess drew Damour aside for a whispered conference. Then she assailed John.

"Now that I have Damour, I have no further need of *your* services, Duke," she said rudely. "He will see us on the rest of our way, and you can scurry off to England."

"Ma'am, the town is full of English, all clamoring for horses," retorted John, realizing that his testing time had come. "In spite of the most strenuous efforts, I have been able to secure only one team, and that I was obliged to purchase. We must abandon one carriage. With luck we may reach Calais tomorrow evening but, if we are all to crowd into one carriage, I fear that most of your packages must be left behind."

"Do not concern yourself, Duke," answered the duchess

loftily, with a disdainful sweep of her hand. "Do you go on to Calais if you wish—or anywhere else. I have other plans."

"That is what I feared, ma'am, but it will not do. You are putting yourself and, what is worse, Lady Georgiana into the greatest danger. Will you not realize that, having missed you in Paris, Bonaparte will continue to pursue you? When his men reach Amiens—and they must be hot on our trail—and find you have not taken the road to Calais, they will easily discover your direction, and it is to Strasbourg that you intend to go, is it not?" John asked bluntly.

"Where I go is no concern of yours, Duke," Jane Gordon blustered.

"You are wrong, Duchess, it is of great concern, but that is beside the point. Precious time is being lost."

The duchess turned her back on him to speak to Damour who stood by passively, apparently unaware of the angry exchange of words.

"Damour, you will make arrangements to escort us to Strasbourg."

"No, Your Grace! I do not wish to disobey Your Grace's orders, but I have more to lose than Your Grace. Undoubtedly I should be arrested and, as a Frenchman, I am subject to the laws of France. I escaped prison during the revolution and have little desire to see the inside of one now. Much to my regret, for the first time I cannot accede to Your Grace's wishes."

John's sigh of relief was audible as he murmured, "Good man!"

Furiously the duchess turned to Sir Harry, whose refusal, though more courteous, was definite.

"It's no good talking to you, Georgiana," said the duchess scornfully. "You're just as bad as the rest."

"Since I am the person most nearly concerned," was her quiet answer, "it is *I* who should have the last word.

We are going with the duke, and Mr. Damour will of course come with us."

Deeply gratified, Damour bowed and left the room to begin unloading the carriage, avoiding the duchess's baleful looks.

At last they were all settled, and the coachman was about to whip up his horses when a distraught figure rushed out of the Lion d'Argent.

"Please, oh, please take me with you! My carriage has broken down and I can get no other conveyance!"

Everyone was astonished to recognize Nancy Maynard. John, with his natural kindness, was attempting to make some room in the carriage, but was prevented by Jane Gordon, who leaned out of the window to shout, "Ye canna' expect any help from me, Nancy Parsons! Ye can go back to the Palais Royal. The general don't interfere with the sluts to be found there, so ye'll be safe enough."

Even Sir Harry was shocked as, leaving Nancy wringing her hands, the duchess bade the coachman drive on.

If the journey to Amiens had been uncomfortable, their progress to Calais was unbearable—the duchess's angry silence was even harder to endure than her chatter. At last, as the sun was setting over the horizon, the spire of Calais's church appeared in the distance.

"Whip up your horses, coachman," cried John in great agitation as the great gates of the port began slowly to close. With a great effort the man managed to extract an extra ounce from his weary beasts, and the carriage just scraped through while the gates clanged behind them.

For the first time in hours John addressed the duchess.

"Ever since we landed, I have had a boat waiting here to row us out to the vessel which has been standing off-shore for us, but I regret we shall have to leave the carriage behind."

"After what has already happened, I no longer expect

any consideration for my property from you, Duke," said Jane Gordon bitterly, looking askance at the skiff in which she was asked to embark. Finally, with great majesty, she did so, to the loud jeers of the idlers looking on.

"*Les braves Anglais!* Scared of Boney, hein? We'll be following you goddamns soon. See you in London, citizeness," shouted one wag in broken English.

Two hefty sailors hauled the duchess aboard the *Three Feathers* and showed her to the cabin below. Sir Harry followed her tactfully, leaving Georgiana on deck with John.

"If John doesn't take this last chance," Sir Harry murmured to himself, "I wash my hands of him."

The evening was warm, with just enough breeze to swell the sails. John was reluctant to break in on Georgiana's reverie as she stood gazing at the land, but she looked around, and hesitantly he walked over to stand beside her.

"In all our helter-skelter, Duke," she said softly, "I have had no opportunity of thanking you for all you have done for my mother and me. Please believe that I, that we, are truly grateful."

"Whatever I have done, Lady Georgy, was as much for my sake as your own."

Would she care that he had acted wholly for her sake? John's great delicacy prevented his saying more, but he continued to stand awkwardly beside her, unable to make up his mind whether to leave her alone or try to rouse her from her melancholy. Clearly her thoughts were fixed on the lover whom she might never see again, and no one knew better than John himself the anguish of parting from a loved one. On impulse he broke the silence.

"Believe me, Lady Georgy, I know what you are feeling. Would that there were anything I could do to help you, but we are faced with the Corsican's insensate ambition. Before he is done he will bring the whole world in ruins about his head."

"At this moment, Duke, I am thinking of one person rather than of the whole world."

"That I understand. In Paris I heard nothing but praise of Monsieur de Beauharnais."

"He merits it. His is a sterling character. He deserves the best the world can offer him."

"Then he deserves you, Lady Georgy."

"You do me too much honor, Duke. I wish that I had been able to return so deep and sincere an affection. I am not worthy of it."

John was puzzled. What did Georgiana mean? He believed her to be deeply in love with Eugène, and that parting from him was the cause of her unhappiness.

Speaking rather to herself than to him, Georgiana continued, "No one could have been kinder than Eugène was to me. I would have married him in spite of—"

She broke off abruptly, and John became increasingly confused. Georgiana seemed to be wishing him to understand something, but what he could not guess. He felt his way carefully.

"Lady Georgy, it is indeed grievous that within so short a time you should have suffered two disappointments, neither of your making, but believe me, you cannot fail one day to find a man who will love you and who will make you happy."

"Oh, no, no!" Georgiana's voice broke on a sob. "I seem to bring misfortune to anyone who loves me—first Francis, then Eugène. Who now would want to marry me?"

"I would!"

The words slipped out almost unconsciously, and John hung his head, waiting for Georgiana to respond coldly or reproach him for his temerity, but she only averted her face. After a pause which to him seemed endless, she murmured, "Would you indeed?"

John had gone so far that he now had nothing to lose by revealing the feelings so long concealed.

"Lady Georgy, I loved you, I think, almost from the first moment I saw you, but I was not free to do so. Then, when my wife died—and I was bound to her by ties of duty rather than affection—you were betrothed to my brother. I had made up my mind to quit Woburn, because to live there with you wedded to Francis would have been intolerable."

A shadow crossed John's face as he recalled that unhappy time.

"When Francis died, it seemed like treachery to think of marrying the woman for whom he had cherished a devotion which was deeper for being less apparent. I could not hope, either, that you cared for me. To put my own fortune to the test when he had just died was impossible. It was only decent to let some interval elapse—"

"I never loved Francis," Georgiana broke in.

"I think at heart I knew this, although at the time I was unwilling to admit it. To me Francis was a great man, my elder brother to whom I had looked up always, eminently worthy of being loved. Only later did I come to realize that you did not share my feeling."

John only just caught the low murmur, "It was my mother's wish that I marry him."

"Yes, I now know how strong is the duchess's will, but then I did not. I had to wait, to reconcile myself to the idea of taking Francis's place, oh, in all things, and by then you had left England. How could I follow you? It was not only that I had so many duties to which to attend; it was sheer presumption ever to hope that you might learn to care for me. Oh, why do I tell you all this now? It can be of little consequence to you!"

"You are wrong, Duke. It is of great consequence to me."

Like the *Three Feathers* nosing its way through the Channel, Georgiana, too, was feeling her way.

John held his breath. Could Georgiana mean that she did indeed have some affection for him? The thought was so dear that he wanted to savor this moment, to remain in a delicious agony of suspense. Slowly and nervously, he stretched out his hand and found Georgiana's. As he pressed it lightly, he was overjoyed by the warmth of her response. Emboldened, he drew her very gently into his arms. Neither knew how long they stood mute until at last John bent and kissed Georgiana's lips. She buried her head on his shoulder, sobbing happily.

"John, John, did you never guess that from the first it was you I loved? When I met you at Charlotte's ball I was so happy because I thought you were the duke and my mother was insistent that, like my sisters, I should marry a duke. Then I discovered my mistake. At Woburn and afterward I did my best to like Francis, but I could not. What could I do? You know my mother—she is determined always to have her own way—and you were married. There could never be any hope for me, so why not please her?"

Tenderly John drew Georgiana down on to a bulkhead as she continued her story. In the cabin below the duchess snored inelegantly, and Sir Harry smiled to himself. If John and Lady Georgiana had not yet made their appearance, all must be well between them.

"When I heard of your wife's death I felt horribly guilty, as if I had wished it, but it was such a dreadful tangle. I was betrothed to Francis, and you kept out of the way. When he died I allowed myself to dream, but when you came to see me you were so formal, so cold . . ."

"My own, my dearest Georgy, how could I be anything else? My mission to you was on my dead brother's behalf. On my part it would have been worse than treachery to obtrude my own wishes, my own longing, and it was too soon!"

"If only you had given me some sign! But you know the rest. My mother took me away. She had a new scheme and I was always merely a pawn in her game. Oh, John, I hope you do not gamble—gamblers get such wild ideas into their heads!"

"You need not worry, Georgy. I am no gambler, which perhaps is why I never dared hope that the dice would fall my way. If you but knew how I felt when I heard that you were betrothed to Eugène de Beauharnais!"

"Poor Eugène!" sighed Georgiana, but almost as if she scarcely remembered who he was, so quickly had John blotted out his image. "Mama was so cock-a-hoop that her gamble had been successful. When she took me to Paris it was with the intention that I should . . . capture Eugène."

Georgiana fell silent, reluctant to admit how far she had returned Eugène's affection but John, who had stood by twice while the woman he loved was promised to another, guessed that one tiny corner of her heart would always be Eugène's. No matter. He was content that the rest would be his.

An embarrassed little laugh burst from Georgiana. "Oh, what will the world think of me, that in one year I should have been betrothed to three men?"

"They will think, my dearest, that all the world must love you, that you are wholly adorable and desirable! Indeed, I can scarcely credit my own good fortune in having won you for myself when there were better men."

John was thinking of Francis, who would always be his hero even if he had not been Georgiana's.

"And," he added with a happy smile, "you are not going to be betrothed to me!"

By the light of the young moon, he could see the look of alarm on Georgiana's face. He stooped to kiss her.

"No, I am not jilting you!" John laughed merrily. "Merely, I am taking no more risks. Just as soon as we get ashore, I shall obtain a special license. We shall not be betrothed but married, and then I shall carry you off to Woburn, which I hope you will learn to love as I do."

"Dear John, you may rest assured that everything that is yours must be an object of my affection."

Suddenly Georgiana sat up.

"But Mama! What will *she* say?"

"My love, your mama will say that her daughter is after all marrying the Duke of Bedford," was John's dry answer. "Not the fifth but the sixth. And I assure you, that she will be well content."

Love—the way you want it!

Candlelight Romances